GREYSON GIBSON'S

# CAPTIVE CAPACITY

# CAPTIVE CAPACITY

*a horror novella*

# GREYSON GIBSON

# CONTENTS

# 1

Curtis stares at the TV screen with an impassioned look. The twenty-six-year-old pauses the videotape on an image of this cartoon character; jumping in mid-air she is. While Curtis' knees are sinking into the carpet floor, soaking in spots of Mountain Dew, marinara, and Stella Artois, he leans forward to press his eyes against the bulb of the television set. He locomotes his pupils half an inch every time he pushes the fast forward button on the VCR. This causes the videotape to only move a frame. Curtis studies, with severe obsession, her outline, and how it moves against her surroundings. He wants to understand the law of physics she is bounded by.

Chomping away Curtis is at that pizza slice nestled in his hand, grease running down his wrist in streams. He's on the sixth slice; the last two resting in the box he ordered from the local mom and pop shop near the community college a few miles east.

Curtis imagines himself in the same position as this character on the screen. However, in his mind, he conceptualizes a box. On the far left he places his apartment complex in a corner and on the far right he places the school in the upper margin, squeezing all those miles in between. To an intricate degree, he is trying to think of jumping from his place to the school in one leap.

But he doesn't just want to visualize it. Curtis wants to understand critically the anatomy in forming this world. How would his body morph from one frame to the next? And would one frame be equivalent to the smallest measurement of time? And would it be to his preference to change the conversion? He could accelerate reality's pace among other things.

Control is what Curtis wants, but he can only do it from his one-bedroom apartment into the drawings he creates. Maybe ten or so years ago, he was comfortable with living within the same four walls constantly. This was because Curtis only lived internally. And during his younger years, the growing pains and spiritual discoveries he experienced allowed his mind to construct itself into a dangerous yet exciting arena. To pull his worlds out onto paper; to illustrate the existence from something abstract and dreamlike to something concrete and absolute birthed transitory highs of attainment and self-validation.

A few times Curtis still even pictures this haze gently wrapping itself over a dimly lit town in the middle of nowhere; its mystifying potency hypnotizing all who slumber in its reach. Those hypnotized are living in fantasies of personal visions and gratification. And from there, Curtis always wants to know each soul who occupies that landscape of his internal picture; who is who and what are they comprised of in a nonsecular way. What dreams and fears do they mask, and can he visit every single intramural world of theirs?

Now, a decade's length has passed by, and Curtis has grown tired of the cyclical nature his mind has become. He feels he's explored the whole landscape, down to every nook and cranny, which constitutes his entire dimension. He wants to transcend way beyond the outline of his body and into what is ubiquitous, energy which is everywhere and takes no permanent shape.

# 2

Curtis, skipping down the steps of his apartment complex, pops his knuckles like soda pops fresh out of the fridge before rubbing them together to maintain warmth against the wintry air. The smell of ash and nicotine along the streets have him cozy up on the inside. Though approaching midnight, the neon signs he's nearing light up a good stretch of distance. He's able to make out a few familiar faces because of that.

"Hey Curtis. How's the comic coming along?" One is asking, slanted against the wall massaging the withering bud of his cigarette.

"Alright. Up to page three." Curtis replies as he centers his eyes on one of many bars in the area, ***Holler and Totter***.

Walking up to the entrance, he is greeted by another familiar person. "Curtis! Haven't seen you in a week." The bouncer, with a merged emotion of amusement and disappointment, announces.

"Owen, you fucker," Curtis fondly says. "How's it been? Thought you moved down to OJ's."

"Didn't pay enough. And they like me here, so," Owen, with folded arms, scans Curtis from head to toe. "Damn, you're still beautiful." Both go in to kiss each other on the cheeks. "Be careful, darling. This place has gotten a tad more aggressive."

"Since they closed down Hidden Spot, of course. Those people gotta move somewhere, right?"

Music of synth and metal blare melodies of youth and dance out all the speakers resting even above the highest balconies. Hands are reaching out for pours of alcohol and lines of cocaine. Spills of even the finest liquor drip down onto Curtis' cheese-stained shirt the moment he strips of his coat. The spread of smoke is so abundant you can mistake a fire breaking out. Well, one is, on the center stage. However, this is a different fire; a fire of desire sparked through that of one's own lack of inhibition.

Three men, each varying in weight by significant margins, are plopped on top of one another like a sundae. The heaviest, only dressed in leather speedos, is sprawled out on the floor sucking face with one bounded by a leather vest and panties; make-up is adorning his face like ornaments would on a Christmas tree. The smallest of the trio, one that is the size of 120 pounds, is riding the middle man to the brink of red skin and sweat one can gulp from a mega-size fountain cup. His harness has a hook connected on the back to allow chocolate syrup to rain down amidst the flashing lights that will go off every two minutes and thirty-five seconds.

Curtis, skipping the bar line, finds a vacant table in the corner; still able to fully view the melting sundae before him. He pulls out his sketch pad and begins to shape the body of the heaviest man on stage. He resurrects hairs that were alive fifteen years ago, and de-ages him. Curtis then takes his pen, and swiftly, at a galloping motion, moves his wrist up and down in tandem to the highs and lows of the middle man's pace. Curtis takes the paper, that practically made of kaolin, and melts the middle one into the guts of the lowest one, unifying and solidifying their intimacy. But he draws himself as the middle man instead.

"Aren't you due for an oil change soon?" Asking a man coming from behind. Turning around, Curtis instantly recognizes who he is. Isaac, the haberdashery showing his age at forty-nine. Consisting of a tucked-in button down shirt, Isaac straightens it out when approaching Curtis. That is Curtis' favorite shirt that he wears, short-sleeved with rounded dots Brailled in a vertical pattern on the front. Suspenders are holding up his jeans, having to extend outward for his XL size.

"Hey there!" Curtis energetically jumps up and kisses his lips tenderly. After, he gives him a big ol' hug. "Sit down. I got no one with me tonight." Both sit down concurrently. Isaac takes a peek at Curtis' drawing while trying to place his Modelo somewhere it won't wet the sketch pad.

Curtis moves his head behind to glimpse at the beige handkerchief in Isaac's left back pocket. "Beige, huh?"

"This is the first time I'm trying it out," Isaac starts, acting like he's just been convicted of a crime. "Some stupid guy said it communicates faster."

"How've you been?" Curtis asks, slamming a quarter of Isaac's Modelo.

"Good. Whatch ya drawing there, bud?" Isaac gives off a strange look at the sketch pad before snagging his Modelo back from Curtis. "Do you need me to get you one, baby?"

"Sure. I appreciate it." Curtis states, part of his attention back on his illustration.

Isaac in turn throws a few bills on the table. "Go fetch it," he smiles rascally. "*Woof! Woof?*"

"Give me a moment," Curtis says while applying the finishing touches on his artistic piece. "I wanna finish this before the next performers rush these guys off stage."

"Is he supposed to be melting?" Isaac questions, stupidly staring at the drawing. "I mean what is this?"

"Symbolism, I guess," Curtis gives an answer, but unsure of it. "They're symbiotic not only physically, but emotionally. They can feel each other's senses."

"You understand that shit on a level I'm not even on," Isaac bobs his tipsy head, downing the rest of his drink. "Do you need me to get 'em?" Isaac brusquely asks, belching out acidic residue from the bowels of his stomach out onto the Brailling of his shirt.

"How early you gotta work?" Curtis wonders.

This causes Isaac to form a cheeky grin. "You wanna spend the night, don't ya?" Isaac, with a boisterous chuckle, bends the joints of his knuckles to better grip his crotch. He eyes Curtis more tentatively the stronger his grip becomes. He starts massaging it to round out the bulge clearly showing through his jeans.

* * *

With a rawboned built, Curtis is waking up all covered up in a queen size bed. He notices an older hand wrapped around his chest, and it's caressing him. He tilts his head behind to see Isaac, the same gruff, heavier set man from the night prior; only thing covering his body are the werewolf hairs grown from the surface of his skin.

Curtis shoots his eyes wide open for a momentary tick, breaking the crustaceous remnants that had nested overnight on his eyelids. Every bit formed like mildew. He stretches his arms, and while doing so inadvertently throws the blanket over on Isaac's side. And suddenly, a glacial flurry saunters on over from the blowing fans directly in front; those fans resting on Isaac's nightstand.

A rowdy clickety-clack of teeth grinding causes Curtis to latch his fingers onto his shoulders. For as little meat he carries on his person, his forearms shield enough of the cold to keep him from freezing over. He uses his nails to dig a hasp into his skin to lock those forearms in place.

Isaac, who had been half asleep, fully wakes to a goosebump-infested spaz. He lets his knuckles, fist shaped, sink into the mattress as he hovers over Curtis. As the crow flies, so does Curtis when he looks up into Isaac's eyes. He excretes this winded sail in a gradual meditation. His body and mind are discharged by his spirited ambitions.

It's not long before Curtis shoots up and amorously grazes Isaac's beard. Isaac then shifts his head with abrasive direction and smooches Curtis, almost looking like an overgrown bass disguised as a hirsute bear. Isaac has a high-octane suction which is cutting off Curtis' oxygen intake, who is suddenly filtered blue in the face. Curtis reaches this glorious high of release and pushes back on Isaac with snogging.

When both men break away, saliva twirls and contorts before splashing amuck when their lips, once again, clash. Their cheeks slap against one another in a tense and puissant hold of their bodies. Breathing in weighty amounts, Curtis is trying to pump air back into his lungs. His face shows this expression of beautiful pain. Isaac slows the both of them down as he kneads the back of Curtis' head, with Curtis pressing up to Isaac's snuggly chest. They both pull warmth; one from the bear's hair, and the other from the twig's now soggy flesh.

Curtis affectionally mumbles, "You're my bear."

Isaac, with ocean blue eyes glistering against the sunrise, eyes Curtis with an inner embrace. "You're my twig," he instantly turns playful. "Little fucker." Curtis laughs while Isaac looks at the clock resting on his nightstand. _9:37_. "And you need to get going." Isaac nudges Curtis while sliding off of him. He then stands at the side of the bed performing stretches. "Shit. You give me a workout."

"You're the one who thrusts like an animal." Curtis puts it back on him.

"And that's a lot for this big boy." Isaac points to himself.

"You do have nice thighs." Curtis is ogling with absolute lack of subtly.

"Oh whatever," Isaac buries his face into the blanket with eyes shut. "Go take your shower."

Curtis, certainly not ebullient, imitates Isaac's slide when rolling off the bed. But the boxers Curtis has on go from square-shaped cotton to a triangular wedgie, getting caught up in the place where the sun _don't_ shine. A sharp ache of his genitalia makes him fumble and plunge to the not-so-cushioned carpet floor. The boxers rip from the splintered daggers of the bed frame.

"_Ow!!_" Curtis wails.

"_Be careful!_" Isaac exclaims. "Are you okay?" He helps him up, tearing more of the boxers in the process. "Liam's coming back today. I gotta run to the market before he gets back."

"You got the day off?"

"Nah. I'm gonna head in at noon." Isaac says, leaving Curtis to somewhat drop enthusiasm. He then gives off this silence, looking like he's jailed in some sort of melancholy. Every so often he'd accidentally lose himself in it. It'd take someone like Isaac to break him out of that cell.

In fact, Isaac notices it and begins speaking for distraction's sake. "More than likely though we'll be closing shop early. They say sleet is supposed to form."

Curtis snaps out of his trance to unveil the curtains over to his left. A beam of sun shoots into his face. "Are you sure?" He questions.

"Give it a few hours. Clouds will form and then it'll hit like the speed of light." Isaac elucidates what he's talking about by mimicking an exuberant noise of roars and explosions. Curtis smiles with a hue of pink scorched onto both his cheeks. He then looks at Isaac moving about, admiring him like a painting. "Hey," Isaac begins. "Could you pass me some drawers?"

Curtis turns, his focus darting from Isaac's breasts to his belly to his calves over to his boxer drawer. However, Curtis is stolen for an instant when his eyes wander halfway up. They lock in on a picture of Isaac wrapping his arm around a man similar in age. But in the photo, both him and Isaac are in their twenties; their smiles expressing a joyful and convivial point in their lives.

"What are you looking at?" Isaac asks after noticing that pensive pause.

Curtis instinctually looks at Isaac, glimpses one more time at the photo, and then goes for the boxer drawer. "Sorry." He apologizes, throwing a pair of underwear in the older man's direction.

"Don't be sorry," Isaac unfolds the pair. "I need to get rid of that. Been nine years."

"Glenn died in '86?" Curtis delicately pursues questioning.

Isaac sighs; that sigh breaking into three with emotional juddering. *"Ye-ye-yeah."* While Isaac drags up his boxers, Curtis heavily concentrates on his own jaw for a split second to shut it tight, feeling a brook of dribble down his sealed lips. He wipes it away quickly.

"May I," Curtis stops himself. "And if you don't want me to, that's totally fine."

Isaac gives a mordant reply to lift up both their spirits. "Tie me up and fuck my ass?" With two hands pressed flat on the now neatly erect bed, he with elvish purpose sticks his butt outward; as if two perfect glossy orbs were trying to break the barrier of his cotton fabric underwear. Perverted yet jaunty moans come about from Isaac, through a smile of lofty eroticism and excitement. His beard curves around that smile Curtis can already feel entangling him.

Isaac, with Herculean labor, vaults over to the opposite end of the bed where Curtis can now smell the after taste of Modelo and cigars. "I'm sorry. What'd you wanna ask me?" Isaac steers the conversation back on track.

"At some point, I'd love to draw you. Like how you are now. Maybe put a Modelo in your hand."

Isaac puts his head down while anxiously nodding. "I'm a slob. It wouldn't be a pretty picture." He then walks out the bedroom door.

"Hey!" Curtis comes off austere making his way along Isaac's path. He grabs his boxers hanging on the chair desk he passes.

The wind blusters with an antagonistic resistance to Curtis' body, knocking him sideways into the arm of one of the porch chairs. Shivers race down his veins with his underwear about to fly off.

However, over to the right of the house is Isaac. Curtis imagines a dichotomy, placing himself on one end and Isaac on the other. Here Isaac is only covered by his underwear too, yet, the sweat forming on his back is whisked away in the blowing wind; a Hawaiian breeze it is to him.

Isaac has his knees bent down to tie the faucet cover on the outdoor nozzle. The wind is blowing a thousand miles an hour and the man is planted like a statue. "This is why I like having just a small, one-story house!" Isaac shouts, his volume triumphing over the squall of the storm suddenly brewing; sun no more. As he gets closer to the porch steps, constructed from wood, he continues on. "Don't have to wrap up too much or heat as much space!"

Isaac limps a little ways up those creaky steps to Curtis, who has himself hugging the front door frame. "You cold, fruity-tooty?" The bear rhetorically asks, gibing at the poor man.

"I'm afraid I'm gonna go flying. I don't have as many twinkies in my stomach holding me in place." Curtis ripostes.

"Oh really?" Isaac, getting all cute, decides to tickle him, having him lose his grip on the door frame.

"*Aah! Stop!*" Curtis takes up a little laughter. "*You're messed up! You know that! You dummy! Slimeball! Stop it you big ol' hippo!*" He waggishly fires off one name after another with a grin almost as round as the Earth.

"Hippo, aye?" A mischievous idea Isaac thinks up. "Where do hippos normally stay, buddy?"

At first Curtis is confused, but gawks when he realizes what that means. Trying to break away from Isaac's hold, the kid is too late when he's lifted into the arch of the man's arms. He starts to panic a little. *"I-Isa-Isaac, wha-what are you doing?"*

"You know what I'm doing," nonchalantly Isaac responds, walking out into the field behind the house. "You better bury yourself into my chest, because that's the most warmth you're gonna get right now." Out there to the fore is a lake which hasn't frozen over yet, surrounded by the deadened trees of the winter's smite.

"What if someone sees us naked out here?"

"We're in the country." The only thing at that point drowning out Curtis' whines were the whines of the wooden dock they were now forging on.

"Liam could ride on in any minute."

"He's gotta teach. He's heading straight to the college. And it's not like he hasn't seen you naked before," Isaac deepens his voice, trying to pull from Vincent Price. "You're trapped my dear. Your fate has been determined."

Isaac rocks Curtis far back then lunges him forward before throwing him out mid-air over the dismal swirl of murky blue and mounds of mushy, shit-colored mud. Curtis plummets into the splashing hooks of the lake's serrated beads, submerged by freezing Illinois water. *"Yo-yo-you fu-fuc-fucking asshole!!!"* Curtis screams shuddering up to the surface.

Isaac shakes his behind before jumping in himself. His splash causes this skosh of a wave, bedabbling Curtis in the face with splotches of mud and what little leaves there were swimming into his mouth. He paddles over and wraps the kid in a tight squeeze. Both can feel the accelerated speeds of their palpitating hearts.

3

Curtis is wandering around one of the halls in the local community college. He is constantly standing up from a bench, looking at an overhead clock, pacing in a circle, and then sitting back down just to repeat the cycle moments later. He eventually walks over to a door and peers through the glass window.

Considering only a few minutes are left of the session, he decides to gracefully stroll in and take a seat in a side chair. Mr. Marlowe, the professor, abruptly stops his lecture and focuses on Curtis. "I'm not done yet. Could you wait a few more out in the hall?" He kindly, but also assertively, insists.

"I'll be quiet," Curtis acts unconcern. "I won't move a muscle."

After giving him a fatherly look of disapproval, Mr. Marlowe continues his lecture with fourteen students as his audience. His stature is that of a bigger construction, similar to Isaac's. His gray turtleneck sweater, hanging over his khakis, compliments his short, crew cut hair—garnished by the sheer color of salt and pepper. He may be fifty-three-years-old, but his looks have their own way of turning back the clock by about a decade or so.

"Let's say two people were to come into this room," Mr. Marlowe begins the closing part of his lesson. "And they take you away because you disobeyed government orders. They take you to a room where they torture you mercilessly until you adhere to their beliefs. Do you still have free will? That's what I want this paper to be about. Is free will inalienable or can it be taken away?"

Mr. Marlowe grabs a stack of papers and hands sections out to the front row. "Pass these papers back. Any extras can be left on my desk at the end of class. This will be due at the end of next week. Minimum of two thousand words and please credit sources. I'm very excited to see what you all write." And like that, class adjourns. Students start talking to one another as they pack and get up.

Isaac then appears in the doorway, with grimy automobile makeup, and makes space for the exiting students before limping on in. Snow dust is drizzling down his faux fur lapel, and the lining is catching much of the drips glissading down his tan gabardine overcoat. Though Isaac's once neatly designed button-up is creased and oily spotted, he makes sure his ties are always permed up. And the one he's donning currently, festooned with cartoonish raccoons, is a classic example.

Curtis stands up trying to fight the traffic after he sees Isaac heading over to Mr. Marlowe, who himself is four-eyed attentive at his desk scaling a skyscraper of lesson plans for the coming weeks. Mr. Marlowe in due course lifts his eyes to Isaac once he passes the white board. Right then he welcomes him. "Oh hey! You get off early?"

Isaac details to him with emphasis, "They say the weather is supposed to get really bad. Black ice," next he leans in with unease on his face. "Liam, I've never seen so much build up. We went ahead and closed up shop."

Mr. Marlowe, or Liam, tries to calm some of his anxiety by suggesting, "Well then let's skedaddle."

Isaac proceeds to rub some of the melted snow off his head and comments, "I'll need to grow hair like you if this continues." He wets the little hair strings he has.

Liam jeers him with, "If you *can* grow it."

"How's your mom?"

"She's alright."

"So, what's for dinner guys?" Curtis blurts making his way toward both men.

"I don't know," Isaac starts off peppery. "Shouldn't the freeloader make supper for a change?" He then buoyantly peeks his eyes to give Curtis a sinister look, all in good fun of course. The kid, shyly, forms a grin; very reclusive to prevent the ignominy of showing blush.

Isaac, acting opposite, lifts him grizzly-like with fantastical growls. Shortly after he sets him down, Curtis sinks into Isaac's overcoat. Curtis' fingers run through the stream raining down his back. For a split second, Isaac scratches and pats Curtis before turning his focus to both him and Liam; every other student having left. "I was thinking we all could head out to the house now. I think we're good on groceries."

Liam, who is fixing his overcoat, aims all his attention to Curtis. "And you're gonna spend the night, too. No need to risk yourself heading back."

* * *

Curtis, Liam, and Isaac are all sitting down at the dinner table surrounding a center pot full of chili; casual conversation going from one person to the next.

"My foot got caught underneath that damn engine. As soon as I pulled away, it felt like I had sprung it." Isaac embellishes a groan when moving the foot in question. Liam nods in understanding while going on to display his stitched knuckle.

"That sewing machine tore my hand up," he says with a mouthful of chili. "So, I feel you."

"How's it doing?"

"Better," Liam swallows his chili. "It sometimes aches to high Heaven still."

"I hope I didn't ruin your class today," Curtis sensitively speaks up. "Sorry 'bout that."

"You're fine," Liam shrugs. "I was practically done anyway."

Curtis suddenly perks up asking, "You still working on that blanket?"

"Yeah," Liam gives a honeyed and treacly smile. "It's taken me a while with the semester and all."

"That just means we can work on it some together."

* * *

Later on in the night, Curtis is sitting down in a corner of the living room, seat pulled up, watching Liam meticulously weave a layered piece of fabric on top of an algorithmic quilt; colors pulling themes of a peacock train rattling.

Meanwhile, Isaac is sitting down in his rocker watching television. The Modelo he's grasping is in a muck sweat, dribbling onto his boxer draws. Curtis looks over periodically and notices the front part of Isaac's torn white T-shirt isn't tucked in; his belly on showcase. He pulls away when he descries Liam's hand in the corner of his retina.

"What technique was that?" Curtis asks, completely redirecting himself.

"I just went under and over." Liam repeats saying.

"How though? I mean how do you not get caught in the fabric?"

"Gimme your hand." Liam commands, and Curtis does so but in a timid manner. Liam rolls his own nails in between Curtis' knuckles. And with marionette-like influence, Liam glides Curtis' hand under and over through the motif of a peacock's feather.

"You make this look easy." Curtis forms this sour look, embittered by the whole process.

"Don't get frustrated, hon," Liam stresses. "I've just been doing it for a while. But I was like you. My mother did this same exercise with me."

Isaac meanders over to them both, Modelo securely fastened, and plops down in the chair next to Curtis. *"What lies are you telling this boy?!"* Isaac shouts with peremptory and gruff intent. He gulps a surplus amount of his sixteen ounce can.

"How to take over the world." Liam plays along with Isaac's tipsy behavior.

"Hey." Isaac nudges Curtis, directing him to Liam. "I've been with this guy for five years. Listen. He's stuck by me through some tough times."

"Did you guys ever try?" Curtis vaguely asks, as sort of a way to walk on egg shells.

"Meaning?" Isaac exhales a nasty odor.

"We never saw each other that way," Liam finishes a small touch on the quilt. "We both needed a place, and this is how we could afford it." And from there, all men leave it.

"Tomorrow's Saturday, right?" Liam asks Isaac.

"I think so," the drunken man thinks for a second. "Yeah."

"Thank God," Liam gives a sigh of relief. "We don't have to worry about going into work."

"That's true." Isaac almost belches.

* * *

Eventually, time puts all but one to sleep. With Liam upstairs, Curtis is left with a snoring Isaac. He's positioned in front of the dulling fireplace sunk into his recliner, not too far from Curtis who's still sitting at the table; this time continuing to sketch his drawing he had started the night at the bar. Though he keeps flipping the page to a new illustration. Who he's drawing on that new one is Isaac.

Every so often Curtis gives this look of swelling eyes at him. A rim of teardrops accumulates in both eyelids; not for any emotional reason, but solely because of strain and lack of blinking. His pupils are being painted darker and darker the more they sink underneath. The wetness is causing this filter of dripping black ink.

Whenever he looks back at his pad, Curtis flips to the original drawing for additional reference. He's erasing the head of the heaviest man, and in place is illustrating Isaac's. The rapid back and forth makes this noise of paper swooshing, which wakes Isaac up. Combatting through his groggy state, he yawns. "You still up, buddy?"

Curtis finishes detailing Isaac's hair and then shuts the pad. "Yeah." He answers monosyllabically.

Isaac cracks his neck on both sides before replying, "Where you gonna crash?" He's greeted by another yawn before digging into his eyes to scrape out crust.

Curtis wanders on over with aimless direction. He sways his body to tumble onto the couch. "I was thinking of crashing here on the sofa." He mentions.

There's a long pause, making time for Isaac to dose off again, which he starts to do. Curtis, still fully awake, sees this and asks, "Would you consider another relationship?"

Isaac opens his eyes and looks outward, seeing nothing but flashing images in his head; those images comprising of his childhood, schooling, military service, Glenn, his job, and now Curtis. This dejection casts a spell over him.

However, unlike Curtis, he doesn't want to wonder in this abstract void that is the human mind. For Isaac, when it does come to succumbing to these mental disturbances, it's not like he can pick up a hammer to fix it. He has to fight to the extremity of outrage to keep these *things* at bay.

"What's wrong?" Curtis asks after a ten-second-long elapse, noticing Isaac's existential stance. He looks like a statue they'd put in one of those art museums.

"I'm tired." Isaac eventually responds, trying to pass off his worried look as an impoverished one.

"Okay. I'll let you get back to sleep." Curtis gives off a slight tone of aggravation before dropping his head onto the pillow beneath him. He knows Isaac's bullshit when churned out.

"I do care for you." Isaac says as a way to compensate for being somewhat bashful.

Curtis, disengaging from the conversation, concludes with, "Vice versa." He then turns out the lamp and they both go to sleep.

* * *

In dreamland, Curtis pictures that dimly lit town dressed in a gently wrapping haze. There's nothing but a desolate landscape beyond the seven only buildings. He focuses on two of the twenty or so residents; one is lying in the bed of a blue and white Chevy C10. He is an older fellow wearing an XL shirt to fit his XL body. He's lounging around the age of forty-five to fifty-five. When he extends his legs out, the elasticity of his lazy shorts stretches to the brink of his drawers showing, and they're hanging on for dear life.

The other gradually approaches the truck who is more similar to Curtis, a younger fellow with a twenty-year difference who has the shape of a meatless skeleton. He's wearing the older man's tan gabardine overcoat as if it's a gargantuan quilt.

The older one is rolled over on his side, completely covered by a quilt bedecked with foxes and birds. Curtis, as the dreamer, thinks back to almost a year ago when he and Liam finally finished a quilt similar looking, that memory agglutinating this clump of merriment onto the younger person in the dream; his eyes, nose, and mouth beautifully decorated. Rising and falling this man's body is who's in the bed of the truck; every once in a while exhaling this almighty snore.

The skeletal one, after stripping down to his underwear, delicately presses his hands and knees onto the vacant side of the truck bed, which has now turned into a mattress. These delicate movements are as is to not disturb the hibernating bear. The younger one gingerly tugs the quilt a couple inches his way, and at the same time allows the mattress to pull him in like quick sand. He rests his head when lying down and faces away from the older one, afraid of waking him up by the odor of his own breath.

And suddenly, he wants to wake the bear up. Out of the blue he has this pained feeling in his chest and an uncomfortable, perturbed haunting of going to sleep alone. He wants watchful eyes over him, giving him consolation and allowing him to escape the pit of his fragmentary imagination. Given the sixty seconds of just lying there, tossing and turning, his mind has jumped from loneliness to disapproval to hopelessness to death.

Curtis jolts up from his dream back into the living room where he and Isaac currently are, where Isaac is still sleeping while Curtis forces himself to do the same.

# 4

"Welcome to Burger Taste, would you like to try our #1 combo?" Curtis recites. "It comes with a burger, a set of fries, and a drink. Best value is the large." Curtis has this smile that looks to weigh a thousand pounds. His face is on the edge of caving in on itself from countless hours of the same expression.

In front of him is a family hurrying to get somewhere: a father, mother, two teenage girls, and an unrestrained ruffian for a ten-year-old boy. Curtis has to keep looking over to be sure the boy doesn't sneak a chocolate bar into his pocket from the rack behind them. A mound of anxiety is beginning to build on the inside.

*'This kid is going to sneak a chocolate into his pocket.'* Curtis is thinking. Meanwhile, the father in front, with hands buried deep into his jeans like he's ready to draw, tips his hat as a way to fidget. Curtis knows the father's fretfulness is stemming from the prices on the menu board. *$12.99* for the combo. *$8.99* for the burger alone. *$4.99* for a drink.

"Jesus," the father bitches. "*Robbery!*" Apprehensively, the father yanks out three crumbled bills; all of them Jackson's. Curtis is having an extremely difficult time maintaining concentration on both the self-riled father and the boy who is climbing all over the candy rack like it's a jungle gym.

'*I need to say something to this man. That he needs to get his kid under control,*' Curtis pontificates while grabbing the bills, trying his best to hide the frailty in his hands. He can never stop himself from shaking once he gets going. '*If I tell him how to raise his kid, he's going to scream and start rambling on about how people like me need to stay out of other conflicts. — No! Stop thinking that. You're just doing your job. You're over exaggerating. — Focus on the kid! Focus on the kid!*'

"…and mayo to three of them." The father finishes.

Curtis has this foreboding, one of which the father is going to strangle him across the counter once he asks, "What was the last thing you said, sir? I'm sorry."

The man, now irked more than before, twitches his eyes. He grits his teeth before intentionally spitting out, "I said I only want cheese and ketchup on one burger, no cheese on two others, and add pickles and mayo to three of them." Sphere-like bubbles, composed of slobber, are being shot at Curtis. These splashes of slime are bombing his face with what becomes an exclamatory rant.

"My God," the man turns to his wife. "And you wanted to come here." Curtis glances at the boy for the fifth time. And he looks back with a smug, a gloating smile that if he wants to, he can steal a chocolate bar and Curtis will be too much of a chickenshit to do anything. Even he notices the sweat beginning to pour down the employee's forehead.

Curtis continues, "The pickles and mayo will be an upcharge of $2.00 for each burger."

The man stares open-mouthed with hostile desire. He allows a tempered jolt to instrument from the root of his throat, "*It wasn't like that before!*"

Curtis then imagines this guy flopping like a fish over the counter to yank him into his reach. Feelings would come over this man unlike any before, feelings of pure bestial rage. He would use his uncut fingernails to scrape Curtis' knuckles, loosening that clench Curtis has on the register to keep from shaking too much.

The rigid points of the man's nails would act as handsaw teeth, gouging the fat in between those knuckles. The nails would be pressed in so firmly that when Curtis tries to move away, they would move in a jagged migration up to his joints where tendons start to tear. At that point, the man, with obstreperous retaliation, would roar in the employee's face while rocketing his own hand into the bottom of Curtis' jaw. With the nails daggered in, the father would begin twisting and creasing Curtis' taut skin into a flabby Twizzler; flavor obviously strawberry.

The man would finally hook a nail through that mighty thick rope of dripping nerves and then anchor Curtis even closer. There he would take the chance to nail him right in what would be a swollen jaw. The kinetic smash would lead to that of fissured bones, causing a sanguinary bidet to rupture from the chiseled shape that would be Curtis' mouth. His body would whump against the shake machine as he remains unconscious for an indefinite amount of time.

Blood would run down Curtis' collared uniform, the red stream forming a circular pattern by flowing down onto all the buttons. These glistening rims would accentuate the blood's thickness, especially when the texture builds and merges on top of one stream over another.

Eventually, Curtis forces himself to snap back into reality and concentrate. Even though his heart is clunking like an old battered machine, having aged fifteen years in the span of fifteen seconds, he analyzes his body for any little motion so he can quickly stop it to appear more confident and composed.

"Actually sir," Curtis cordially starts to respond. "We've always had these upcharges. I'm sorry that you feel this way." *Curtis wasn't sorry.*

"Not a few weeks ago," the father argues back, obviously making shit up. "You're just a fucking liar. Next time I'll bring my own goddamn drinks."

'*Oh, please don't let there be a next time.*' Curtis internally begs to God.

"And yet you don't lower the price when I want to take things off." And there the man goes storming off with his family. The boy sticks his tongue out at Curtis not even hiding the candy he just stole. Curtis takes in a deep breath, easing his nerves after realizing the entire line finally dissolved.

∗ ∗ ∗

In the back, Curtis is mopping the kitchen floor, getting the teenagers ready for the night shift. '*Thank God I work first shifts on weekdays.*' He exhaustedly reflects, ready to snap his mop stick in two.

The front entrance bell goes off, and that can only mean one thing: another self-righteous, entitled little shit can scream and bellow his life problems at an underpaid staff member. Curtis glimpses at the hand clock above the manager's office. *3:55*.

'*One more hour. Just one more hour. And then tomorrow, another eight fucking hours.*' He tries to reboot making his way out before completely turning gleeful. Isaac is standing at the counter having gotten off work, holding a container of brownies bought from the local bakery shop.

"Hey there! What's up?" Curtis excitedly gallops over to him.

"Nothing much." Isaac, almost in a shy way, lowers his head, as if taking note how the kid became instantly glued to him.

"Are these from that shop across the street?" Curtis asks, already knowing the answer.

"*Yeeeah?*" Isaac expands his eyes out, making it seem like the most brainless question had been asked. And because of that, nothing is said in response for quite a bit.

"Well, Liam wanted me to get you these after I got off work." Isaac explains. Curtis can hear his own heart deflating like a balloon, and it fastens his chest into a stiff slab of concrete. The wind is knocked out of him for a good moment. "You okay?"

Curtis sometimes gets annoyed when Isaac asks that. Because when he does, Isaac sounds like he's obligated to do so, and that there can only be one answer, and that Curtis better answer in a matter of seconds.

"I'm fine," Curtis replies deadpan, trying to speak in code for: *No, I'm not you shithead! Why couldn't YOU have bought these for me?* And what really gets Curtis is that Isaac knows his language, and will not engage with his passive behavior. "How was work?" Curtis acts mindless and apathetic, attempting to transform himself into a mirror.

Isaac yawns, "Work." And that's it.

"Got it." Curtis pretends to yawn.

"Um," Isaac begins with a more sensitive tone. Curtis drops his act at a stroke, looking at him with locked eyes. "I was talking to Luis. He works at the shop. Around your age." Isaac starts whispering, "And I tell ya, he's drop dead gorgeous. He's the one who can't stop staring at me."

Curtis' eyes slump, bowed down with a gloomy drear of tired bags. "Yeah?" He responds with humdrum tedium, continuing to mop.

"Would you want to head over to his place after you get off? He's okay with you tagging along."

"I'll pass." Curtis is hoping, even though he knows the rules of the game, that Isaac will see his friend's subliminal plea. That plea being: *I don't want you to go either.* Instead, this nauseating concern of disconnect is imbued with awkward silence.

'*I just wanna say I love you, Isaac.*' But Curtis doesn't want to sound desperate, and he doesn't want to shackle him to a relationship. Again, he knows the rules of the game.

"Okay," Isaac drops back to his monotone delivery. "I'm gonna go ahead. I'll see you later?"

"Yeah." Curtis shuts his lips tight after breathing out a watery mumble.

# 5

"106, 206, 207," Curtis is talking under his breath while directing his finger from up to down, and then left to right. He finally finds his mailbox. Good old number 208. He inserts his key and unlocks the miniaturize vault to find a pile of mail.

One is a check from Burger Taste. A whopping sum of $513. At the end of the month, he could average a little over a thousand. But, about half goes toward monthly rent. And from there, about a third for groceries. That usually leaves him just under $350 if he averages 35 hours a week, which he usually does.

*'If I deposit another hundred into my savings, that'll leave me…* *$121? Shit. Maybe I'll only deposit fifty this go-around.'* Sure, it makes him depressed glancing at his bi-weekly checks, but Curtis is determined to remain strong. Persevere until he gets accepted and published… *oh wait,* his next envelope contains a rejection slip.

Dear Mr. Murray,

We have looked over your submission for our newsletter. Unfortunately, we must pass on your comic strip, *Tobi and Talla*. Don't let this discourage you. We can only select a limited number of the many submissions sent in. So please, if ever you want to submit again, you will be welcomed with open arms just like before. Be sure to submit a payment of $100 to be considered for this amazing opportunity.

Best wishes,
-Daily Post Newsletter

A long sigh escapes the recesses of Curtis' stomach. He quickly flips to the next envelope to use as a divergent to avoid melancholy and sorrow, and the next one is definitely a judder of excitement.

Dear Baby Bro,

I hope you've been merrily. John and I sure have. And that's because he proposed to me last month! Yippie!! I'm expecting you to be there, Butthead. As of right now, we're not sure when the wedding's gonna be. But I'll write to you well in advance. And don't worry about dad being there. I didn't invite him.

Also, Beatrice keeps asking when "Huckle Curtis" is going to visit. It's been too long. Wish you all the love there is plus more.

Love,
Big Sis Gwen

Curtis walks up the stairs to the second floor where he enters a musty, war-torn bunker as he imagines it to be; pizza boxes trashed over in a pile next to his 1980s Toshiba television set. VHS tapes are scattered throughout like medical supplies thrown all over the place. He sits down in a chair, one clawed horrifically from his neighbor's cat. But hey, at least his neighbor Rhiannon gave him that chair for free.

Curtis masks his face with the palm of his hand, hiding from everyone including himself. Shame is all he feels, no matter what he says otherwise. Next, he turns his head to the rotary phone on the bar table, which is sitting on the outskirts of the kitchen–3 yards in length and 1.5 yards in width, including the stove and mini fridge.

The man stands up with a half-baked idea. *'A forlorn escape from the rapidity of my ever-dwindling time.'* He thinks as he cups the phone in his hand. No matter who answers, one man comes to mind without fail. After waiting many rings, on the other line Liam answers, "Hello?"

"Hey Isa…" Curtis cuts himself off, embarrassed by his mistake. "Hey Liam. Is Isaac there?" Curtis expects a response like, *'No, he didn't come home.'* Or… *'Sorry hon, he left not too long ago.'* Or worst of all… *'He's out fucking a co-worker he's had his eyes set on for a while. I mean, he's single Curtis. Do you really expect him to hold down a relationship, you fucking idiot?'*

Curtis snaps out of his ridiculous and hyperbolic imagination when Liam starts repeating himself. "Hello? Curtis, you there? Hello?"

"Yeah, sorry about that. Where'd you say he was?"

"In the shower. I'll let him know you called," Liam says. "Is everything alright?"

"Um," Curtis just wants to spill his guts. Yell aloud all his frustrations. "Yeah. I'm calling him about a trip down to Tennessee."

"Is your sister fine?" Liam asks with the gentlest voice, most genuine as well.

"Everyone's doing good. I was just wanting to ask him if he'd like to tag along."

"Oh," a long pause ensues. "I'll tell him to call ya back."

"Thanks."

"Not a problem, hon. You take care, ya hear?"

"Yes. I hear." The line disconnects.

* * *

Curtis puts a frozen pizza in the microwave for five minutes. Chemically processed marinara starts to sizzle about halfway through. That is Curtis' cue to pour himself a glass of cheap, red wine. Though he'd knock out a fearsome portion with just one glass, that glass starting at a line of sixteen ounces, he wouldn't balance his diet with his alcohol intake, or pace himself for that matter.

*GULP. GULP. GULP.* Damn he feels goooooooooood. After two small pizza slices and a whole wine bottle later, a resting squiggle of gaiety lies firmly upon his face. He walks around his living room in circles thinking of flashing images; those images turning into movement, and movement being directed into one hallucinogenic arthouse film.

In this film, flashbacks are shown of a father grasping the hair of his baby boy. These slides are soon drenched in dripping red lunacy as the father screams and throws his kid against the wall. This causes a stream to race down from the back of the child's head to the floor where it builds up a mound of shiny fluid.

Curtis, back in the physical world, suddenly turns horrified. He begins to rapidly breathe in and out. He wants out… out of his head. The merging of shapes disorients his vision, burying him beneath the surface down into the core of his broken psychology. He races back to the phone where he dials the most recent number. Over on the other line Liam responds again, "Hello?"

"Li-Liam? Cou-could you come over?" Curtis stutters as he places his hand on his forehead. "I don't feel right."

"Do I need to call 9-1-1?"

"No. I just drank too much."

"Stay put. On my way." Liam reassures.

"Thank you." Curtis hangs the phone up.

* * *

"My mind is everywhere." Curtis, with vibrating quivers, responds as he opens his front door for Liam. He gives his head a rubdown to massage the headache that is slowly, but surely, coming on like a spiritual possession.

"I want you to sit down," Liam instructs. "Sit down and try your best to relax." Curtis' thoughts are beginning to race again, as if someone is driving a Corvette who dropped a brick on the gas pedal. What makes it worse is that he doesn't have direction to guide the vehicle. Crash can happen at any moment.

Liam closes the door and puts both his hands on Curtis' shoulders, steering him over to the center couch. There, once he gets the kid to sit down, Liam sets his water bottle over to his right and covers Curtis' body with a quilt that had been folded behind them for nice décor.

"Do you remember when we made this one?" Liam starts, referencing the bedspread strapping Curtis' body. The kid looks down at the sharks and fishes sewn all over.

"Yeah," Curtis drunkenly sways his head to collapse onto Liam, the kid using his face to fiddly nuzzle against his chest. Curtis' eyes go up and down, clearly showing how uncoordinated he is in this moment. "We made it shortly after we got together."

Liam replies, "We did." He looks around the apartment and sees point blank the pigsty surrounding them both, his face showing a disgusted reaction.

Meanwhile, restless and irritable, Curtis opens his eyes and zeroes in on that quilt. *'Is the blanket covering all of my body? Yes. Yes, it is. Stop it.'* Curtis' thoughts are faltering, each one hastening that process. His breathing becomes hyperventilating. *'I can't function. Oh God, I can't function! This shark here,'* Curtis embarks on another thought, scoping the quilt more obsessively now. *'The shark isn't aligned with my feet. The quilt is positioned more diagonal than straight.'*

Liam's water bottle over to the right makes a loud pop from the dent it once had, the bottle rounding itself out. Curtis is vexed by that as well as the blowing fans. They're getting louder and *louder* and LOUDER!

Curtis jumps off the couch pacing to the door, back to the couch, and to the door, and back to the couch, over and over again; his pace and breathing accelerating. He's on the verge of gripping his chest about to scream out, *HEART ATTACK.*

*'That's what I want right now. I want a heart attack. I wanna feel nothing. I wanna die. I suck. I'm a horrible person. I'm a fucking failure!'* That last thought knocks him to the floor against the door, like being hit with a strike of lightning. Tears come about as he sits there, on the carpet with knees up to his dimples, which are forming because of the tormented smile he's making. Finally, a nauseating jerk of movement has him fully blubbering.

Liam hops off the furniture himself and bolts hell for leather over to Curtis. He, with aching joints, kneels down before plonking his buttocks onto the carpet floor next to the kid.

"Calm down," Liam emphasizes his own breathing intake. "You got this." Liam, like one of their quilts, wraps Curtis with radiating love. He brings him in with a big, wet kiss to his forehead. "You're just having another episode." Liam then takes Curtis' head and holds it like a book looking face down directly into his eyes. "You got me?" Liam speaks with a dictatorial timbre, but it being out of positive reinforcement.

Curtis doesn't say anything. All he wants to do is just listen, or at least the best way he can. By responding to Liam, he simply nods with a fainthearted reception. His lips have sealed shut taking on the shape of another squiggle. However, this one birthed from suffering. His teardrops have reduced to the pace of just scathing down his cheeks roughly every ten seconds.

"I love you very much, Curt." Liam affectionately says.

"*I-I feel li-like I'm,*" Curtis stops because of an aggressive hiccup. "*A fucking idiot.*"

"Why?"

"I can't function."

"All you have is an imbalance." Instead of replying, Curtis strengthens his hold on Liam.

# 6

"Why does he go back and forth?" Curtis asks Liam, both of them now sitting at the dining table in Liam and Isaac's home. Though he's still a bit sluggish, enough time has passed for Curtis to somewhat sober up. Liam is sitting there staring out into space. He takes a minute before replying.

"That's who he is," he answers vaguely. "I don't know how else to put it."

"I hate how close he gets," Curtis respites his sentence then, trying to restructure his wording. "I don't like how intimate he gets with me, and then pulls back completely."

"He really does feel for you, hon," Liam takes a drink from his water bottle. "A relationship is hard for him."

"Why though?" Pleading, Curtis looks earnestly into the other man's eyes. "What isn't he telling me?" Unfortunately, all Liam is doing is shaking his head without reciprocating that eye contact.

"He's hurt."

"*By me?*" Curtis assumes, instantly turning defensive.

"No." It's obvious Liam is cautiously going in slow motion when he speaks, as if trying to meticulously say the right things at the right time. Nothing else is spoken for a long minute.

Curtis glances down and scoffs. "He never called me back."

"He was in a hurry." Liam defends, trying to keep the peace.

"You told him, right?" Curtis gives him that earnest look again, but more in a subtle fit of rage.

Liam is still, not even making thuds with his feet. He digs deep down to pull a very guttural, monosyllabic answer. "Yes."

Now not so subtly, that fit of rage makes Curtis clench his fists, tightening his skin to display purple veins moving like circuitry and wires. "He doesn't *fucking* care!"

"Stop that!" Liam barks back. "You're gonna get yourself riled up again."

"I feel like I'm just a placeholder. *Jesus!*" Curtis claws down his face before Liam grasps his wrists and pulls them away.

"Please calm down," Liam begs. "That is one thing you've never done away with since we've been together."

"Is that why you broke it off?"

"You ended it with me." Liam unwaveringly opposes. Curtis goes hush hush after recognizing that he's right, and this happens immediately after his pushback. "But that's alright. You slept with Isaac after the fact."

And speaking of, the unbolting sounds of the front door catches both their attentions. Isaac, looking downtrodden, slumps in with a scorn from the netherworlds; his face producing the most terrifying grimace. Curtis flinches a little, even with Isaac so far back under the door frame.

"How you doing?" Liam directs his tone more host like, trying to welcome in this slouchy grump of a man.

"I can be better." Isaac growls, teeth bared. He doesn't even look at Curtis when making his way passed the dining table up the stairs. Once they both hear Isaac's door slam shut, Curtis gets up.

"I'll head out. Could you drive me back home?" He asks, that being a euphemism for: *Rescue me from this asshole.*

"Stay," Liam commands. "I don't want you alone tonight. You're still sobering up."

"I've sobered up on my own." Immediately after saying that, Curtis realizes that sounded more wrong than right.

"I worry 'bout you sometimes," Liam relaxes his cheek on his knuckles. "Both me *and him.*"

"I don't have my work uniform…"

"We can go get it." Liam interrupts nonchalantly.

"How'm I supposed to…"

"I'll drop you off. It's not a problem for me."

* * *

Curtis is sitting in their living room working on that peacock quilt after having picked up his work clothes. He is the only one awake. Though he's drained of more energy this time around, having spent the evening wasted out of his mind, he still has this push to keep going, never ridding his fear of time.

Down the stairs, however, comes Isaac, who at first is in his own world. He then shifts his head slightly to glimpse at Curtis, this hint of a smile locks onto his face as he charts a path into the kitchen. Curtis chooses to not follow that path. In fact, he decides to not even acknowledge the bear rummaging through the fridge.

Though peace be damned as Isaac walks back into the living room with a PB & J sandwich and a glass of milk. "How far along are you?" He caringly asks, putting out a gesture to bury the hatchet.

"Over halfway," Curtis starts, trying to keep his eyes focused; not so much to keep concentration on the quilt, but rather, not to give Isaac too much recognition. "Hoping to finish it within a month or two."

"You have really taken that and made it your own." The bear continues, using that as code for: *I'm sorry I've been a douchebag.*

Now Curtis' mind is in an intermediate stage. Does he accept his apology by turning this monologue into a dialogue, or does he simply quilt on in silence? How much can he push the envelope without losing Isaac again? Then he thinks, '*Why do I wanna push this? He wants to reach out and make sure I'm alright.*'

"Thank you," Curtis raises his head, accepting the apology. "Under and over as Liam would say."

Isaac gives a slight chuckle. "Yeah."

Curtis resumes focus on his sewing, allowing for quietude to enhance the now good morale that began circulating the air a minute prior.

"I want to be with you." Curtis blurts without thinking, as his thoughts would've kept him silent.

Isaac gives off a neurotic exhale, trying to play off whatever was just spoken. "You are with me. You and me are sitting here right now."

"No. I want to be your partner. Your boyfriend."

"You don't want me. I'm an asshole. I'm impulsive…"

"So?" Curtis isn't even registering those words: *asshole, impulsive.* "I like you."

"I like you, too," Isaac is about to say it; Curtis is waiting to wince on the inside once he hears it. "*BUT…*" And there it is. BUT. Not Isaac's butt unfortunately, but one T–B.U.T. "We'd be rushing into things."

"*We've known each other for four years!*" Curtis exclaims.

"Shh," Isaac uses his hands to indicate their volume needs to lower. "As *friends.*"

"We've slept together," Curtis argues. "A lot."

"Does that mean Luis and I are together then?" Isaac suddenly becomes snooty, as if he had this in his arsenal ready to use in case of–*EMERGENCY: Curtis is acting all bitchy.*

But Curtis grows out his claws and roars twice as loud. "So, you and Luis have done it multiple times. I see."

"That's not what I *fucking* meant, ya shithead." After Isaac says that, Curtis keeps to himself for a few seconds. This puts the kid in a gloomy state. Isaac, colder than ice, stares him down with almost slits for pupils.

There have been times Curtis was nervous around Isaac, there have been times where he'd been frustrated with the guy, and there have been times he felt sorrowful. However, this is the first time he sees something utterly terrifying. Isaac's face indicates he's on a *until further notice* recess. His glass of milk rests on the table with a quarter left to go, but more than likely he won't finish it, probably forgotten it.

Honest to God, Curtis feels he's going to be murdered by this person, by this thing possessing his friend's body. He will end up in the newspaper as a young man whose life was tragically cut short by a looney tune who yielded a household kitchen appliance. It takes him a second to toss his jitters.

"I'm heading back to bed." Isaac concludes. No—*Coming with me?* No—*Are you staying up?* They both know something is off, and they both know the other knows something is off. One big, gigantic elephant is stinking up the room with unpalatable omens. Isaac stands up, gathers his balance, and maintains a slouch to keep that balance while heading back up to his room.

"May I join you?" Curtis dreadfully asks, knowing the answer already.

Isaac doesn't stop, doesn't even turn to face him. "There's room on the couch."

Curtis leaves it there. Isaac though mentions one more thing: "And it's best I don't go with you to Tennessee." And that's where he leaves it.

# 7

A streak of orange splashes against the sky's gloaming, creating this dazzling image of a bright neon array. Night is quickly drawing upon the skyline, and Curtis is on his third iced espresso from the third stop in his long drive to Tennessee.

*'Just as long as a work shift,'* he keeps telling himself. He wanted to leave earlier, but Burger Taste had too many patties on the grill. *'I'll be there by midnight.'* He thinks while looking at the time on his dashboard–**_8:28pm_**. *'Why don't they ever come up to Illinois? – Stop thinking that way. You're the one who wanted to see them. – But it seems they never make the effort to come up and see me. – Again, stop thinking that way.'* He's making animated expressions while mentally jogging the perimeters of his mind, something he tends to do cyclically if you couldn't tell by now.

Inevitably, he throws in a cassette. What comes on is contagious rock n' roll. He instantly syncs to the twelve-inch extended version of *Who Made Who* by AC/DC. Once the lyrics start to play, he sings them in tone-deaf screams, deliberately trying to stay awake. Instead, his screams drown in watery mumbles that taper off due to sleep deprivation; or in layman's terms as Isaac would ask and Curtis mouths an answer, "*STRESSED THE FUCK OUT*", as if he's answering Isaac who he wishes is in the passenger seat next to him.

* * *

The time is 12:17am when Curtis walks up the embedded gravel road leading to his sister's house. *KNOCK. KNOCK. KNOCK.* He waits a minute given when he's arriving, but the door does eventually open. There John is in a white T and boxers. "Curt, how the hell are ya?" He welcomely invites him in.

"I'm alright," Curtis dawdles in, centering on good conversation. '*Finally, another face.*' His mind tells him. "Sorry about being a little past my time."

"When were you supposed to be here?" John asks, looking at the grandfather clock in the entry way.

"Midnight."

"Shit man. Don't sweat it," John pats Curtis on the shoulder after locking the front door. "Twenty minutes ain't a damn thing."

"I don't wanna wake Beatrice though."

"See, you're already doing it." John, in abnormally high spirits, points at his wife's brother endearingly.

"You seem cheerful for being up this late."

"Dude, I couldn't sleep," they make their way into the kitchen. "I've been in and out, but that's about it. You want a drink?" This is something Curtis misses. When he lived down in Tennessee, he always had a pal to go drinking with… well, a pal to go drinking with who he didn't want to bone. They could shoot shit and not give a flying fuck about anything except the kind of whiskey they preferred.

"Make it a double. Marker's Mark." Curtis responds, looking around to place his bag down.

"You can just set it in the living room." John says, pouring what appears to be more than a standard double.

"Don't get me too drunk now." Curtis takes a seat at the kitchen island.

"You probably need it after the long drive you've had." John slides the drink over, and Curtis elegantly takes a swig like Isaac would. "Who you with this time around?" John continues, sitting at the island alongside.

"Fuck if I know. Liam and I haven't been together since May of 1990," Curtis lets out a monster cough after the whiskey coats the back of his throat. "And I can't figure out Isaac for the goddamn life of me. He's guarding himself for whatever fucking reason."

"You and Liam were together that long?"

"A year and a half."

"I'm surprised you two survived that."

"We were fine together. Isaac just knew how to schmooze." Curtis looks out into space with a concerned look, as if thinking how the hell did he end up here. "He came in saying the right things. Was physically intimate. Now it's every once and a while does he get a fix, and with whomever."

"Have another." John exhorts after taking his empty glass.

"You really are trying to get me drunk." The two of them laugh in a very bubbly way.

"I've been dealing with bull all day. I haven't needed to get this bad in a long time," John goes for the bottle again and out comes the medicine. He doesn't even pay attention to how much is going into their glasses this time around. "We got into a little fight."

"You and Gwen? *Noooo*." Curtis sarcastically says before taking another gargantuan swig.

"You're gonna be an uncle two times over. She's pregnant again."

Curtis conjures up another monstrous cough, and clutches his throat to better maintain it.

"It'll be fine," John calms him down. "It's just that we did it a little ways out before the wedding." John, more methodically, takes a few gulps as if trying to better time his drunkenness. "I don't know. I can't afford another child, Curt."

Neither of them ever feels that three-year gap they have on each other, and that makes John feel not as old. Curtis brings him back down to twenty-six, and the bottles de-age them to those entering their twenties. They're kids again.

"I got something to show ya." He nudges Curtis.

"Seen it."

"And you're still jealous."

"Fuck off." They both give off those bubbly laughs again, this time bouncier and rowdier.

"But actually, I came across this thing." John wobbles on his feet and motions Curtis to do the same.

Out on the back porch, Curtis hangs over the gated ledge while John runs out to his shop. When he returns, one hand is gripped tightly. "I couldn't believe it when I tried this." John mentions, directing the attention down at his closed, cramping knuckle.

"Dude, I thought you would've tried fisting by now?" Curtis guffaws, still in that smartass realm both occupied not too long ago. However, John is somewhere else entirely now. He forms a face of momentous occasion, and opens his hand to unveil a substance of blue sticky residue.

There it is with a base, and out from that base are two sprouts shooting up. One sprout is a sunflower yellow, and the other is an alien green. Quite the contrast Curtis thinks, in addition for how small it is. "What is it?" Curtis asks in a straight, blunt fashion; anything playful having vanished from their aura.

"They say this has the power to take God away from you." John emphasizes, having heaved those words very carefully.

"You tried it?"

Instead of answering him verbally, John steps aside. He steps aside to show someone has just appeared out of thin air. It's a man in his thirties who has on dirt-encrusted shoes. He has on a torn TCU shirt half-ass tucked in to his begrimed shorts splotched with what looks to be black sludge.

Judgment would say he was attacked and taken against his will; his face horribly bruised and body awfully scuffed. All this confirmed when he starts to scream: *"HELP ME! I CAN'T MOVE!"* And the man is right, he can't. Plain as day, or night in this case, he tries and tries to make so much as one creak on the porch, but simply can't. And then, he vanishes. Fades out in less than a millisecond.

'*Hallucination?*' Curtis blinks stupidly.

"That was real." John answers his friend's thought, knowing what he's thinking.

"*You did that?!*" Curtis grows even younger, acting like a kid who's just learning his ABCs. "*What the fuck just happened?!*" Even swearing like a child.

Again, John demonstrates as opposed to explaining. The man fades back in, still screaming. *"The neighbors are going to hear, John!"* Curtis yells.

John gives him a slight smack on his head. "The only thing they're going to hear is you yapping back here. Only we can hear him. In fact," And there goes his sound. All that can be seen is a jailed mime. "Not even we can."

Dumbfounded Curtis is. John sees this and begins to ease the tension by explaining, "This guy tried to ransack Gwen when she was out at a gas station. Thankfully some people were walking by when he approached her, so nothing happened but just a little struggle," John points. "This piece of shit managed to get away. But I tracked him down. And one night while he was jogging, I attacked him."

John moves his head slightly up and the man in turn fades out, and then fades back in. This time, out on the back lawn. "Watch this." John says. He has this jovial look seeing this guy bounded by his logic, his time, and his reality. The guy's shirt stretches; the fiber ripping into tiny shreds as his chest becomes bare. The big blots of dirt explode in his face when his shorts go poof. And his briefs split in two, leaving him butt ass naked.

*"STOP IT!"* The man exclaims, still muted. But it doesn't stop. He gets shoved to the ground, and his legs are being pulled in opposite directions by an invisible force, by something John is controlling. The cracking of bones can be heard unitedly with his shrills of aching pain, that pain now going up his chest in a single red line. His chest hews by an unseen weapon, causing a splatter of blood to shoot across the freshly cut grass; the two main colors of Christmas decorating the area. Bits and pieces. That is all that's left.

The back door swings open, and there Gwen is in her nightgown. "What are you two doing out here?" She nosily asks. She's standing in a spot close to where Curtis is, where the spread corpse is on full transparent display. But she pays no mind to it, as if she can't see it. "How was the drive?"

"*Gooood?*" He responds, sounding not so confident.

"Are you okay?" Gwen shows this concern, noticing the pale paint dressed all over Curtis' face. Sweat is rolling down his temples.

"Yeah." He spastically answers.

"You guys started for that Maker's already." She nods her head with askance.

"Curt doesn't come around too often," John rationalizes. "The occasion is right."

"Past midnight?" She questions, and no one says anything after. "Don't stay up too late now." She goes in to kiss John, and then heads back inside.

"*She didn't see it!*" Curtis yells in a tight whisper.

"Of course she didn't. I kept it from her." John theatrically states. Curtis looks out at the body again, cueing John to get rid of it. "Oh, sorry." And it vanishes, all of it; the torn ligaments, scattered veins, blood puddles, anything that is anywhere goes poof.

"Where does it go?"

"It stays in my head," John takes in a deep breath. "He lived in there for a good number of days. I'll be glad to finally erase him during REM."

"As in REM sleep?"

"Yeah," John joins Curtis over the gated ledge, showing that two-headed sprout again. "I got him with this. I drank the yellow juice, and forced him to take the green. After only a couple minutes, he was mine."

"Yours?"

"Correct. Mine. His being. His existence was entirely dependent on me." John begins to twiddle his thumbs after a long pause. "He deserved that."

"How much?" Curtis comes out of the blue very blunt.

John gives this abrupt turn of the head as even he didn't expect that, at least so soon. "For what?"

"Don't play that. You fucking show me hocus pocus out here. You know what I'm talking about."

"How much you looking?"

"How much you got?" Curtis slows himself down. "Wait, will I be having the FBI at my doorstep?"

John laughs. "Why would the FBI show up at your place?"

Curtis gives a look of: *Are you stupid?* "Will they?"

"No."

"Where'd you get this?"

"All these questions." John paces on the porch figuring how to spell it out.

"*John.*" Curtis demands, getting impatient and nervous. "Where did you get this?"

"Gwen doesn't know about them," he prefaces. "They're a group from our church. They're the ones who supply these."

"That doesn't answer my question." Curtis gets in John's face.

"Fuck man, get off me. I can smell your breath." He shoves him a few inches the other way. "Wolf River. Particularly in the ghost section. That's where this shit's found. I don't know how it's grown, picked, or anything."

"They just give you this stuff?"

"We have a mission. And one of my duties is to find people."

"What do you mean *FIND*?"

"Our mission involves the worlds inside ourselves. This one out here," John peels off a piece of the porch gate. "Is falling apart. Physically. Morally. You name it." He holds the drug out for demonstration again. "This gives us a chance to create the worlds we want, and to correct those who make life difficult. I want you to test this out and see for yourself. I'll give you five."

"I'm not comfortable with this. You just ripped a man like shredded cheese."

"I know you, Curt. You have these strong visuals, firm beliefs, and an understanding for measurement. You can help us, and we can help you. There can finally be authority and order."

# 8

Beatrice darts down the hall screaming how a seven-year-old would on a Saturday morning with no school, and Curtis hears this beyond the guest bedroom door. '*Static on the radio would sound much more pleasant.*' He gets up and doesn't bother to look at the time. A three-time knock is conducted on the other side, and he moves to get himself dressed.

"Breakfast." Gwen announces when he opens the door.

"On my way." Curtis yawns.

*BOINK, ZIP, POW.* That is what's playing on the TV in the living room. Beatrice is running around mimicking her animated programs when Curtis passes by. "Huckle Curtis! Look! I'm Huckle Cat!" She pretends to have claws for fingernails.

"I see that." He gives off a playful hiss, which makes her chortle with a cosmic smile. Curtis proceeds into the dining room. John is pouring OJ in all the glasses while Gwen is finishing up the eggs by dumping them in a communal bowl.

"Sweetie, I'm not gonna say it again after this!" Gwen yells, but gently. "Time for breakfast!"

The stomping of feet races over to the table, having carried Beatrice with them. She has a troubled look on her face. "Momma. It came back on."

"Baby, we need to eat together, especially on weekends. Daddy set the VCR to record."

"Always do." John inserts, trying to ease the pout forming on Beatrice's face. She slumps down in her seat not saying a word.

"So, we have some news Curt…" Gwen starts, her excitement showing prematurely.

"You and John having another kid? I know." Gwen's cheeks collapse and her eyes produce this particular scowl Curtis used to get when they were kids, whenever he would make her smell his shit-scented finger. Curtis looks away to create less awkward tension, but to his left is John who is giving him his own hyperbolic reaction. Code for: *You're supposed to act surprised.*

Curtis puts two and two together when she aims her frustrations at John. She asks in a distressed sort of way, "*You told him?!*"

"It slipped. We were drinking a lot and stuff came out," John exaggerates. "I got really excited thinking about it." The doorbell goes off, and this causes an awkward situation to turn into an overwrought nightmare.

Curtis takes a sip of orange juice when he hears the distant voice of his father, and he coughs quite a bit back into the cup. Gwen had opened the door and from there, dad's voice lingers closer and closer. Curtis races out of his seat as it increases in volume. He becomes panicked. His chest swells up and his skin profusely leaks sweat.

"Dad," Gwen has an anxiously driven tone to her voice. "What are you doing here? You usually call."

"I was driving around and wanted to stop in. There wasn't a payphone nearby."

"You know there's the one next to the library." She explains, but like that's going to do much now. Dad is here, and Curtis is queer. A good stretch of distance between several states kept these two from starting World War III.

Curtis is getting ready to sprint when John goes, "Calm down man. What's he gonna do?" This keeps him from leaving the room, and instantly regrets it when that voice, now directly behind, triggers the deepest recesses of his memory bank.

"Curtis. How are you?" Something that simple causes an earthquake to erupt inside Curtis' stomach. He grips his belly and squeezes it like one does to a towel wringing out water.

*'Just turn around. You're a grown man.'* Curtis tries assuaging his nerves. He eventually turns around after spending a few seconds composing himself. "Hey dad. I'm good. Thought I'd spend a day or two with Gwen."

His dad passively chuckles under his breath. He stands there with a flannel button down shirt tucked into Wranglers, glossy leather boots with a sharp finish, and four fingers resting downward in both of his front pockets. After both men say no more, he pays mind to Beatrice who seems the happiest to see him.

"Pops!" She feverishly scampers to hug the side of his hip, and he tries his best to return it without exerting too much energy given his age.

"How you doing, hon?" His smile is a bit torn from his timeworn furrowed face.

"Meow!" She exclaims, acting all animated again.

"Are you a cat?" He lovingly plays along, flailing his arms as if he's in a cartoon himself.

"Meow!" She goes again, this time pawing at his face.

"You're a little booger! Has anybody ever told you that?" He rhetorically asks, and she giggles with that missing tooth beam.

"May I go watch the rest of my show?" She innocently blinks her eyelashes.

"Go for it, hon." He rubs her hair before she bolts back into the living area.

Gwen forms a face of agitation toward her dad when she spots Beatrice's plate still has a good number of eggs left. "We're trying to teach her to sit down and eat her food."

However, dad points to his son with a smartass retort, "Apparently you need to teach this one as well," he says, referencing the escape Curtis tried to make. "There was only so much I could do."

"Leave him be, Mr. Murray." John chimes in.

"Hey you," Mr. Murray starts in warmly. "How the hell are ya?" He proceeds to shake John's hand.

John gives a warm reception by laughing cordially, and then awkwardly when looking back at Curtis. "Good."

"How's the station?" The old man asks with full interest, taking a seat next to the all-American husband Curtis thinks disdainfully.

"Alright. We got a new DJ. Been training her to take over Mondays for me."

"Hopefully that'll give you a third day off." Mr. Murray pats his knee affectionately.

'*If dad were to pat mine,*' Curtis pontificates, staring at them both. '*He'd think I would enjoy it too much.*' He then catches himself staring and moves away. '*Don't stare at them. You'll make him feel uncomfortable. – Fuck, why do I care? That's his problem. – He wishes he had John for a son.*'

"That's the dream, right?" John replies genially, taking a drink from his OJ. Curtis has had enough and simply walks out the front door. Gwen is the only one who follows after him.

Curtis is having trouble seeing with the sun blaring in his eyes, but still marches forward with confused determination. "*Where are you going?!*" Gwen yells after him, the screen door slamming shut as she runs.

"You didn't tell me he was coming." He bitterly tells her.

"He showed up unannounced." She explains, catching her breath.

"I didn't know you were still talking to him." He scornfully says.

"*Of course I do!*" She screams back. "And you will not put me down for it. It's bad enough I can't invite him to the wedding."

Curtis takes a moment, his right cheek twitching from poked nerves. "I'm sorry. That wasn't right of me to say. That in there was getting to me."

"If I had known he was coming, I would've told you."

"I know." They both calm down.

"You still heading out?" Gwen benignly asks.

"Probably up to town. Kill some time. I just don't wanna be around *him*."

"That's fine. I'll page you once he's gone. How's that?"

"Alright."

# 9

The land stretches wide, displaying a wide selection of pasture. Connected to it is a trail, one that a ten-year-old Curtis and his father are currently on. By Mr. Murray's side is a bucket of feed enough to take care of all three horses.

The ground is squishy with puddles scattered throughout. The rain just a little while ago had really come down like a busted fire hydrant. Curtis wraps himself steadfastly when a drizzle begins to form. His father, though, extends his arms outward in a cross shape; the rain acting as some sort of baptism.

Curtis can tell he's clearing his mind; something his father does consistently, maybe even every day. "I don't want you to get behind Hannah," Mr. Murray instructs. "She can get a tad bit mean."

"She kicked you at one point, right?" Curtis asks.

"And it hurt a hell of a lot, let me tell ya." He concludes. "Now, after this we're gonna weed eat some of the overgrown shit. And as soon as that sun shows itself, we'll put some new hay out."

"Yes, sir." Curtis answers back, respectfully. Around the corner, in the horse shed, is Impulse. He's occupying the first of three stalls. Both guys don't need to fret as much with him. Impulse is usually a calm one. Only time he ever shows signs of aggression, or aggravation, is when you're disturbing him while he secretes his mouth in a mound of feed. He'll give you ten seconds to back away once you drop the last crumb in his rusted feeder, hanging up on the wall by twenty-year-old screws, put in by Mr. Murray when he was a twenty-year-old screw himself. It wouldn't be for another ten years after he put in those screws Curtis was born. Good old year of 1966.

Curtis and him make their way to Layla's stall. Now talk about gentle. This horse has a high emotional intelligence, it's almost supernatural. She's a therapy horse; one who nuzzles her nose against a scraped knee, one who senses bouts of depression and will give you the look of salvation, one who will stand in front to shield you from the numbing wind. A keen observance she has.

"So why are you failing math?" Mr. Murray, in a somewhat macho tone, turns confrontational.

Curtis' hands shake from the sudden loss of balance. His legs always get weak when his father flips that switch from unassuming to antagonistic. "Um…" Curtis drags on, abruptly forgetting the feed he's pouring into Layla's feeder, all from this instant blockage of trepidation.

Layla politely nudges Curtis, lifting the bucket with her nose so as not to pour anymore. "Pay attention when you divvy that out. *God damn!*" His bellicose father has officially lost himself to hostility.

Finally, the myth and the legend of Hannah. Hardly ever did Mr. Murray allow his children to step so much as ten feet within her perimeter. Mood swings possess her with every breath inhaled. Curtis avoids anymore eye contact with Mr. Murray, and has this resting bitch face when beginning to pour the bucket into Hannah's feeder.

"*Drop. The. Attitude.*" His dad dictates, the veins in his eyes now popping what can only be described as red dye, but it's thicker. In fact, it's straight up blood. The red backdrop, contrasting with his golden pupils, creates a distinctive image Curtis will never forget. This is the genesis of what would become an ongoing case of ommetaphobia, the extreme fear of eyes, for him.

The look into a person's rings, at its core, is the naked semblance of soul. Yet, Curtis is drawn to them. As one would be drawn to spiders with a case of arachnophobia or drawn to underwater ships with a case of submechanophobia. There is this incredible fear of something alien that puts him in a state of wonder and curiosity.

And his dad always senses it; a component of the human experience that can't be faked. Theatrics are mere paradoxical. One cannot overreact or play pretend. Fear is one we cannot run from; it is one emotion we cannot calculate through. The utter truth will show for itself without fail.

*SMACK!* The collision of Mr. Murray's palm against Curtis' thick skull occurs just seconds after his dictatorial words. "*Answer me, boy!*"

"It makes no sense, dad." Curtis responds, sounding short.

"You're telling me I've stayed up late," Mr. Murray raises his tone with every few syllables. "Been late to work. Tired throughout the whole day… just for you to tell me it makes no sense?!"

Curtis goes silent per usual, finishing up the bucket. And Mr. Murray sees his son's deliberate head turn, causing him to raise his dried, wilted fingers. He motions the kid over to him. *"Come here you little shit."* And Curtis does so.

Like a spider clenching its prey, Mr. Murray takes his wilted fingers and grabs hold of his son's entire head. *"Aaahhh!!!"* A scream all too real is evoked, its echo reaching landscape to landscape when his father takes his other hand to give poor Curt an Indian burn hotter than Hell itself.

"I'm gonna be sure your sorer than I am," Mr. Murray states with a violent but albeit gladsome approach, as if taking sick amusement from his boy's pain. He quickly turns deadly with Satan's voice on full orchestra, *"You're gonna feel the strains work puts on me."*

Across the stall Curtis flies, his shoulder dislocated from impact of the dividing wall. His dad stomps over after him stripping his belt clean off the rim of his jeans. Repeated whacks of the barbaric kind fall upon Curtis' bruising skin, concocting a delicious and vibrant color of bleeding organs. His skin goes from scuffed to red to tearing, and his father keeps going.

Blood sizzles on the leather belt, and the speed at which Mr. Murray is striking his son expedites. Even faster *than that* it seems to be going. Curtis goes from, *"Aaaaahhhhh!!!!!! Dad!!! Stop!!! IT HURTS!!!"* to a whimpering, *"Ah….!!"*. His fortitude is no more as he goes down for the count, lathering in his glazing blood. He soon wakes up in his bed having aged back to twenty-six and soaking in a lake of lukewarm sweat.

He glances his eyes around to familiarize himself with his surroundings. He had returned home a few days ago, and keeps mentally repeating that to break his convulsing jitters. '*I was only dreaming.*' He's fatigued. After a whole trip down to Tennessee, seeing estranged family, and cycling through nightmares, who wouldn't be. '*And then there's that drug.*' He tells his conscience.

Curtis bends and stretches before standing up, and even then, he stretches some more. '*Shit. Am I really getting there? It seemed like a millennium away getting older.*' His eyes adjust once he turns the bathroom light on. He grabs one of the drawers and pulls it out, and there they are. Five tiny blue membrane cells as Curtis thinks them to be, all in their coated slime. How John described them, they'd have to be a sort of membrane; there's immense power and it's housed somewhere.

"*Those two sprouts that shoot out the base,*" Curtis is recalling a memory with John, who did try to explain the best he could. "*The yellow one is the dominant juice. The green is the submissive part. The victim has to intake that stuff while the controller intakes the yellow. Give it a few minutes and the person will dissolve into your mind—into your world.*"

Curtis takes one of the pieces with him into the bedroom, and examines every centimeter while making his way back toward the bed. He recalls more of what John said, "*It's called the MIND DRUG. All they will be anymore is a figment of your imagination. They won't be bounded by real world physics, nor by God directly. You become their God.*"

"*Will they still age?*" Curtis asks John in his memory.

"*No. Well, not by real world logic. If YOU want them to age, or de-age, they can. If you want to change their appearance, you can. They won't have to eat anymore. Nor sleep. Nor breathe. Nor anything until you change the rules. Remember, they are a part of you.*" John says, that last sentence spoken with a guttural histrionic.

"*What about death?*" Curtis continues.

"*They don't die until YOU die.*" And that's what attracts Curtis most of all. "*There is one down side, and that is you can't break into their psychology. You can twist and contort what's physical, but you absolutely CANNOT manipulate their mental makeup. Who they are is who they are.*"

Curtis asks in response, "*Can I so much as see what's in their head?*"

"*No. Not to my knowledge. BUT… they can see what's in yours. They will be able to explore and discover everything that makes you the person you are.*"

He hasn't quit looking at this thing as he sits on his bed. His mind breaks away from the expository dump and cinches a decision that will, he believes, set him on the right track. '*I need to test this out.*' He thinks while putting on gym shorts and a shirt, having placed the Mind Drug in a pocket size container.

**10**

'*He's too big. Easily can get away.*' Curtis is analyzing every guy he passes among the crowd of people in a not-so-usual gay bar of his. In fact, he's never been to this one at all. It sits on the far outskirts of the next town over. The reasoning is simple, and he learned it after watching a few shows of *Unsolved Mysteries*. Go to an area far away where nobody knows you. Really, it's an elementary formula. And he likes imagining the voice of Robert Stack for amusement.

He sits down and orders a double shot of Tito's with tonic, a repulsive drink he finds it to be. However, he doesn't want to order anything traditional, something that would announce *CURTIS WAS HERE*, no matter how small or trivial the movement may be. Strategic and calculating he outwardly becomes, scanning the room for body shapes, personalities, and those who are on an island as opposed to hanging with a group of friends, or *wanna-be* hook ups.

He soon stops, and rewires his face once he begins to approach a man looking to be in his thirties drinking alone. "Hey!" Curtis hovers. "May I sit here!" He asks, amplifying his voice to a high degree as to be audible over the electronic synthwave blaring from side to side.

The man at first looks timid, but after a few seconds, pulls a chair out as a return gesture. "Go for it."

As Curtis sits next to him, the hunt for this particular prey commences. "You with anybody tonight?"

"No," he answers, wallowing in a splash of his drink, as if thinking nobody to get in his way of a hot twinkish guy and himself. "Are you?"

"Nope," Curt answers back. "My name's Will."

"Stu," the guy holds his hand out and Curtis shakes it. "What are you drinking?" Stu carries on, looking at Curt's cup of Tito's not even a quarter drank.

"Tito's and tonic."

"It doesn't seem you like it all that much," Stu observes. "Let me buy you something that really gets people going."

"Nah. I'm just pacing myself," Curtis quickly interjects, trying to prevent Stu from moving another muscle out of his seat. Next, he looks at his drink, a Screwdriver more than halfway empty. "You know that's better in the mornings."

"I've been told." Stu plonks down in his seat drunkenly.

'*He's already almost there.*' Curtis thinks.

"Let me get you another one though. In fact, I'll get one myself." Curtis deceptively puts out there. And Stu doesn't respond at first, but eventually answers with a slight nod.

'*Usually, I'm the one people are trying to get drunk.*' Curtis continues to monologue in his head as he marches over to the bartender with an important purpose, or so he tells himself to justify what he's doing.

* * *

Stu stumbles into Curt's apartment, and behind him the door shuts tight. Charming Curtis leaps for him with an "*affectionate*" hug, encasing him how Isaac would, and Liam for that matter.

"You feel so good." Curtis falsifies a moan, causing Stu to turn around and touch lips with him. They migrate over to the couch, Curtis making sure he has the dominant force. Once settled, he sneaks the concealed container out of his pocket; Stu being distracted as he locks tongue. Curt sexually rubs the stem of Stu's throat, making an inconspicuous attempt.

'*Give it a few minutes.*' Curtis recycles John's saying as he gets closer and closer to enacting his plan. '*I can't believe I'm gonna drug someone. – Don't overthink it. Just do it.*' His conscience is in the middle of a civil war. Inevitably, one side perseveres. Curtis lightly squeezes Stu's bristly throat, and with riotous maneuvering, jams his hand down the mouth. There, a slight pressure from the pressing of Curt's fingers makes the green sprout explode into a drizzle before outright pelting the esophagus with a clump almost as thick as pus.

A violent *COUGH* takes over, forcing Stu to catapult remnants of alcohol and saliva onto Curtis' now clenching fists. While Stu recovers, Curtis studies his hands with tremendous detail to ensure none of the juice shot back up. He even forms a small case of buck fever thinking he might've squeezed the wrong color, but has a huge sigh of relief when he yanks out the second sprout to find it is indeed the yellow one. He pinches the lump, and out comes a shiny liquid shooting straight into his own mouth and down the throat.

"*Who the fuck do you think you are?!*" Stu wobbles onto his feet and punches Curtis in the blade of his shoulder.

"*OW!! Fuck you!*" Curtis caterwauls, giving Stu a disgusted look. But he returns the same feeling with his own facial reaction.

"*Fuck you!*" Stu then uproariously steps his way over piles of miscellaneous crap, having his hand reach for the incoming doorknob. *BUT HE STOPS*. His body turns stiff with sudden muscle rigidity; his face now wearing an expression of unbearable pain. One finger on his extending hand goes *SPLAT*, having plummeted to the floor like mushy cake batter.

He turns to face Curtis, and there isn't a readable expression at all anymore. Curtis screams, and then Stu screams. They both scream because of the ice cream texture his skin is turning into. "*Whud-you'd-to-mee?*" Stu is finding it difficult to annunciate. Rather, each sentence is now starting to sound like one long, disjointed word. He's also growing shorter; his legs are melting like butter. His upper half soon topples over into a splatter on the floor that shoots far ranges around his perimeter.

Stu, though, is still conscious, and enduring unspeakable agony. He looks to Curtis, who's looking back with both fear and amazement. Stu's gurgling screams become lyrics against the backdrop percussion beat of gushing blood. The man who's now turning into cherry flavored spoiled milk emits a faint whimper, ululating over his now melting torso.

"*It... sss...*" Stu forms a stuttering cry from mangled-like tonsils. "*They're gonmmm...!!!*" That one jolted wail shoots clods of massacred muscles from the back of his throat, composing another gurgling sound. He can't even taste his tears rolling down into his mouth, splashing on the gory balloon he has for a tongue; each slit tearing wider from just one tiny stretch. It eventually explodes with an almighty *BOOM!*

'*Rocky Road anyone?*' Curtis nauseatingly imagines. All down to a repugnant mound of membrane mush Stu has turned into. And after staring long enough, Curtis pukes. The vomit falls in heavy clumps onto the carpet in discolored green.

A stream begins to float upward from that mush, however, and lines up like stardust. An asteroid belt of Stu's remains seep into a force field now being projected from Curtis' forehead. Its glow powerful enough to blind those that look directly into it. Curtis is in a state of momentary paralysis, only catching the outer edge of that glow before it goes away completely. And from there, Stu has completely vanished as well. The place appears to be as if nothing went on the last few minutes.

Curtis carefully stands up so as to not trip or fumble. He feels a glob of sweat across his forehead, slime having been produced from something bright and incomprehensible. He shifts his head side to side trying to locate Stu. He closes his eyes and tries to search for him in his head, and nothing.

'*What am I even looking for?*' He covers his entire face.

"What did I just do?" He asks himself aloud. "*Did I just fucking murder someone?*"

* * *

Curtis is restless. He tosses and turns in bed as the time hurries from one minute to the next. Soon, it goes from 4:00am to 5:00am to 6:00am. Little slices of sleep here and there, but nothing uninterrupted. He finally doses off just from pure enervation.

And the town sits where it always does–in Curtis' dimension. But for this go-around, instead of looking through the eyes of first person, he allows himself to be viewed in the third person. He walks the streets glimpsing at the people who he's seen countless times over. Then, someone new. No, someone familiar who moved into town not too long ago. *STU.* Curtis sees him running up as he was seconds before the consumption of the green juice. Skin and body fully intact. Wholly clothed. Simply altogether.

Stu comes running toward him with a sharp fist ready to slug him six feet under. And Curtis doesn't know how, but a subconscious reflex permits him to be cloaked downright ghostly. Stu's punch flies right through him and into the glass window of a barber's establishment. Stu stands up with shards of glass resting firmly in between his knuckles as blood runs down. Curtis, by invisible force, holds Stu utterly still and heals his hand by removing the shards and repairing his skin like nothing happened.

*'That seems to be a running theme, don't it?'* Curtis tells himself. *'Like Nothing Happened.'*

*"Let me go!"* Stu cries. *"I don't know where you've taken me, but LET ME GO!!"* And that's just it, Curtis can't. He harks back to another response John gave him.

*"Can you relinquish them back into the world?"* He had asked.

*"No,"* John wasn't completely confident in that answer. *"At least, I'm not sure."*

*"There has to be a way to give back if we're taking something."* Curtis concludes his flashback. And he's confused on

where to go next. Does he keep Stu here? Yes, he's going to have to.

# 11

Curtis is restocking large cups on a model day of work. To his side is Joey, who is changing out a trash can almost filled to the brim with greasy wrappers and condiment-stained napkins. "Another Wednesday, right?" He pessimistically comments to her.

"Tuesday." She corrects him, and Curtis dons this frown when showcasing her a temporary glance.

"What's wrong?" Joey persists, and he gives off an ill-mannered attitude. As if non-verbally implying that is an idiotic question that she very well knows the answer to. She senses this, and goes full blast. "You seem unhappier every time we work together." She creates a violent prominence with the knot she's tying on that trash bag, stirring up her own non-verbal reply of: *You will not look at me that way.*

"I'm getting tired." Curtis gravelly states. And then a gust of wind holds the front entrance doors open, and following after is an old chum from a couple weeks back. This time he's alone, without his family, and appearing as pissed off as he was that day.

'*Maybe his son didn't share that stolen chocolate bar with him.*' Curtis humorously thinks. The customer storms over to the vacant register, and Curt urgently rushes behind the counter manning his station. "Would you like to try our #1 combo?" He asks, going off the script.

"Burger. That's it," he plainly states. "Keep it simple for you this time."

"The works?" Curtis espies his name tag pinned to his work shirt. **DIRK**.

"Cheese and ketchup." And like shutting the tail end of a book, the transaction finishes. Curtis is surprised it went by that smoothly. But this is only the transactional stage. Will his burger be cooked to a medium level of red and juice? His family isn't around to domesticate him. Curtis, however, realizes the moment Dirk walks off that he can "*mistakenly*" pour him a soda pop.

'*Will the green show?*' Curtis filters his thoughts making his way out to his car with a powerful impulse. He begins to devise a plan while searching through his glove compartment. Four mind drugs lay in a perfect line, in a container able to house them all. He snatches one and makes his way back inside.

* * *

"Here you go, sir." Curtis sets the basket and Styrofoam cup down.

"I didn't order a drink." Dirk says.

"Oh, you didn't?" Curtis theatrically bulges his eyes out. "I'm sorry, sir. Force of habit. You can keep it if you'd like." After a few suspenseful seconds, Dirk motions his hand for: *Just get the fuck away from me.*

Curtis trails back to the counter where he had been restocking those cups, waiting to hear that of slurping from a wild boar. '*I'm not enjoying this,*' he then starts fighting one thought after another. '*He won't die. I'm needing to do this. Stu didn't deserve that, but this guy sure does.*' Curtis stares into space, unaware he's over stocking at this point. '*Frogs and cats are dissected every year at Grassyfields High School. Science–IT'S SCIENCE.*'

*SLUUUURRRRPPPP.* There it is. No more squabbling over moral quandaries. It's time to sit back and watch the show. *PUMP. PUMP. PUMP.* Curtis is racing to finish stocking, but fumbles here and there with a case of juddering. The final sleeve collapses to the floor in a cluttered spread.

"You need help, Curt?" Joey calls for him, aiding to the rescue.

"Um… yeah." He can't feel anything, not even the thuds that are beating his chest. He can't bear another horror shock show. "I gotta use the restroom. I feel I'm about to pass out."

And before Joey can say, "I can take care of this", Curtis is already sprinting. He slams the stall door once in the bathroom and lowers his head. '*I'm not a bad person.*' He takes the yellow sprout and chomps down, almost tasting like a tart strudel with the most heinous sour there is.

Meanwhile, Joey cleans up by storing away the remainder of the cups. The cabinet door closes with a thud of its own, in tandem with yet another thud; this time coming from Dirk who strikes the table with a bay as loud as a dog getting mauled to death. "*AAAHHH!!! IT'S BURNING!!!*" Staff and customers are claimed alike when pure panic smacks all their faces.

Curtis is traversing his legs from the toilet to the tiled wall back to the toilet. He hears lunacy breaking the sound barrier over on the other side. "You're mine, Dirk." He chokes under his declaration just then.

Out on the floor, Joey and two customers scurry to Dirk's assistance, grasping lumps of butter. One clenches Dirk's face, which trickles through the gaps of his fingers. A swirling blend of red and beige coat all their hands and arms like they're bathing in a massacred bakery. Toddlers are wailing, mothers have their arms flailing, and others are bailing. Absolute pandemonium.

In the restroom, Curtis' forehead begins to smolder before a glowing flame finally sparks through rupturing tears. That flame forms a circular shape, and unleashes a formidable gravity that terrifies those out on the floor. Just like with Stu, Dirk's remnants float up into a perfect stream and are glided as if travelling through a siphon with a suction as powerful as a baleen whale.

The flowing line dives underneath the gap of the bathroom door and upward into the force field radiating brightly from Curtis' forehead. *SMACK!* He gets sling shotted, banging his back on the wall tile behind. He goes unconscious.

# 12

Eyes jolt up, and Curtis finds himself in a hospital room resting on a slab of concrete they call a bed. He's attempting to regain what's what, and trying to figure out if he had been in a coma and just experiencing a prolonged nightmare. As he rests upward, his back bends and pops. He makes out one–no, two people: Liam and Isaac. A reestablishment right then almost makes him cry. Everything makes sense again.

Curtis doesn't hesitate to jump up, no matter how pained he is, and hooks both men into one merging squeeze. Liam follows with, "They wouldn't let us see you at all yesterday."

Usually, Isaac would go on a tirade to further cement the injustice of the situation. Not this time, though. He takes in Curtis even stronger than the kid had done to him. The older man starts sniveling before a hiccup sets off a wave of sputum and bawling.

"What happened guys?" Curtis faintly asks, assembling energy.

"They found you unconscious at work," Liam explains. "One of your co-workers had apparently said you were on the verge of passing out. Like you looked ill or something."

"*I don't want you working there anymore!*" There's the tirade Isaac is known for, finally. "*It was the food!* Did you eat anything that day? From that piece of shit restaurant?" Isaac grips Curtis' face.

"Yeah, I think so," Curtis pauses, recollecting. "Just a burger…"

"*That's it! That man ate one, too! It killed him! And it almost killed you!!*" Isaac, in simple terms, loses his shit. Anybody could understandably assume murder was taking place in there.

"You're gonna get him riled up," Liam tells the hysterical man. "You're not doing him any favors." He comes off more and more short tempered, having bags under his eyes from the pressure of stress and anxiety, and has shown to have lost a good few pounds rather quickly.

"Who are you talking about?" Curtis plays dumb. "Who got killed?"

"You're not worrying about that." Liam says, as if disciplining one of his students.

"When can I go back to work?" Curtis comes off with a certain frailty, needing to cup his stomach and hold it in a particular position to ease soreness.

"*You're quitting!*" Isaac yells.

"First, you need to lie here and rest," Liam doesn't let up. "Then once you're back on your feet, you may start looking for something else. They're shutting down that place until further notice."

Curtis raises his arms as if surrendering. "Okay guys, I understand," he rolls his eyes. "I feel nauseous, and that my head's gonna explode any minute."

"Do you need Tylenol?" Isaac asks, which makes Liam thinly hit his shoulder. "*Ow.*"

"We need to check in with the doctor first." Liam stresses.

And it's as if the doctor hears him because there, she comes strolling in dressed in scrubs. "You're awake, Mr. Murray." Her tone is an uplifting one.

"Did you have any doubt?" Curtis jokes.

"Stop that." Liam dourly dictates. The doctor turns to catch a glimpse at him, and then back to Curtis.

"Not at all," she grabs a stethoscope and presses on the patient's chest. "Please breathe in…" *INHALE*. "Now breathe out." *EXHALE*. "Again?" *INHALE… EXHALE*. "Can you follow my finger?" She continues, holding up her index in front of his eyes. In a straight line, Curtis moves his pupils without any dizziness or handicaps.

"He'll be good to head out today. Are you taking him?" She nods her head side to side acknowledging both Isaac and Liam.

Liam speedily raises his hand in mid-air. "Yep."

"Be sure you drink plenty of water," the doctor lists out. "You'll need to take it slow. Tomorrow is all in the house, and then you can start venturing out. And please control your caffeine intake." She adds.

"Yes ma'am." Curtis relaxes after she gives him space.

"I'll get you ready for discharge." She concludes, walking out the door.

# 13

Curtis is five years younger. He and Isaac are almost to Gwen's house, she and John just rooming together at the time with Beatrice only two-years-old.

"His name's John?" Isaac asks, having driven he and him in his own blue and white Chevy C10, model year 1977.

"Yeah." Curtis answers, his arm flying out against the push of the autumn wind. Isaac deaccelerates the vehicle after turning into what looks to be a hybrid of rural country and suburbia. Houses lined up, but far and widespread enough to where each piece of land can go three acres at least.

"What number again?" Isaac nudges a distracted Curtis who's looking out at the passing tree branches. "Hey, what number?" He gets a little short.

"Oh," the kid acts as if he's waking up. "Sorry. It'll be three more houses down. 316." He keeps pointing until Isaac nods his head in understanding. They inevitably pull into the driveway.

Up the embedded gravel road they walk. Before they get up to the front porch, the door flutters open. And there Gwen comes skipping out, excited she finally gets to meet the fantastical, grizzly Isaac. "You made it guys!" She goes from skipping to sprinting, nearly tackling Curt to the gravel and pinning the man. After she pulls off, her and Isaac give one another a formal hug, and then she suddenly clutches both his butt cheeks.

"*Ooh!*" He lets out a high-pitch squeal.

"*Damn! He picks better men than me!*" Gwen jests loudly, mashing both orbs in a tight massage.

"Thank you, thank you very much." Isaac conducts an authentic belly laugh, his smile applying structure for his dimples to hold up his glasses. Good thing his cap, albeit a very faded brown showing its age, is blocking out the overhead sun searing down like a fire breathing dragon.

Gwen had taken his damp cargo shorts and crinkled them into a disaster. What was once neatly tucked in, his sweat stained tractor T-shirt made of a suffocating cotton, is now hanging over the border of those shorts.

'*Get your mind out of the gutter!*' Curtis gets on to himself after Isaac raises his arms, stretching from the long car ride. The twenty-one-year-old has a difficult time snapping himself out of an erotic trance, especially after detailing a stream running down into Isaac's visibly showing boxers. His arms finally go down, covering his underwear with the drenched shirt. '*What is wrong with me?*' Curtis thinks to himself. '*Dad won't be too pleased.*'

Curtis turns away, wandering about the property while sister and friend get acquainted. He buries hands in pockets slumping from one broken down golf cart to another. "Yeah, I gotta get to those eventually." He hears

John's voice out by their diminutive pond, the man sitting under an awning hanging over a miniaturized dock.

"When?" Curt responds, making his way over and sitting next to him.

"At some point."

The crinkling sound of leaves becomes higher by the passing of seconds. Soon, within reach for the two of them, is Isaac. "Hey John." He holds out his hand, and John shakes it in return.

"Hey. Nice to meet you," he points to Curtis. "He told me you two have been going since July."

Isaac blinks his eyes in a state of discomfiture, making it even more awkward when he gives Curtis a spoiled look, and the kid stutters in response. *"W-we-well?"* As if signifying: *We've been banging.*

Peering beyond Curtis, Isaac corrects John cordially. "We're just friends."

"I'm sure I just misheard." John says as a way to remedy a cumbersome situation, but the stone is cast.

"What do you do?" Isaac abruptly interjects to distort the quieten effect the last sentence had on them.

"Radio station." John simplifies.

"So, you're the one who's *Goooooooooood morning, Vietnam!*" Isaac fondly calls upon the voice of Robin Williams.

And John forms a grin, even a little chuckle. "Not quite. They say I gotta work at least a year. Get familiar with what's going on behind closed doors."

"You make it sound top secret," Isaac mimics a smoking motion with his index and middle finger. "You got any?"

"My wife." John counters, licking his lips sexually.

Isaac larks by sticking both his fingers in his mouth, repeating the motion one would use eating a popsicle. "I play for the other team, buddy," he teases on. "We could draft ya."

"I'm pitchin' then."

"I prefer it." And while Curtis is giving off a vibe that he's uncomfortable, the other men are too much in their own fun to notice. They pat each other with uproarious gestures and clangorous banging. "You and Gwen are already too much." Isaac warmheartedly remarks, his laugh tail ending his comment.

"Yeah," John jumps back to his last question, pulling out a carton of cigarettes and a lighter. "Right here." He mentions while handing the older man a lit stick.

"Thanks baby doll." Isaac licks the side before his first ingest.

"Where's Gwen?" Curtis asks to sound courteous, but in reality, needs her to be his savior.

"She went inside to get Beatrice," Isaac answers, inhaling smoke like he's never taken a breath in his life. "It's been eight *loooonnnng* hours."

"Eight long hours of breathing in actual air?" Curtis flings a riposte back at him, coming off aggravated. And Isaac's face is morphing into an ugly one before interrupted by an impression of a baby's voice.

"*Yeeesss. There they are,*" Gwen is walking toward them holding Beatrice in her arms. "*Uncle Curtis and his partner.*"

"Should you really be saying partner around her?" John worriedly asks.

And Gwen's voice switches to a steely tone. "She's two, you dummy." Saying that to more so preserve her brother's feelings. But Curtis has a bigger problem when Isaac gives him a downright scowl.

"It's fine. We're not together anyway." Isaac coldly states.

* * *

"When's dad gonna be here?" Asks Curtis, who is opening two packages of candles; one **5** and one **1**. He firmly sinks each candle pillar into the chocolate icing on top of the cake.

"He wanted to stop by Savannah's," Gwen explains, her attention split between setting up the table and attending to Beatrice in her high chair. "That'll give us more time anyway." John and Isaac are heard conjuring up loads of laughter in the other yonder, and Gwen has a mumbled sigh.

"Everything good?" Curtis inquires.

"Sometimes I wish he'd do a little more," Gwen answers, referring to John. "He sits out there all day and comes inside just to do the same thing."

Curtis divvies out an equal ratio of paper plates to placemats on the table, and then solo cups. "Do you think dad will take it well?" He asks her.

"I hope so." She rests her elbows on the counter and uses her hands to massage both temples.

And next, he stares into space with overwhelming trepidation. He beseeches to her, "Please don't leave the room for whatever reason."

She turns to face him. "Why do you wanna tell him on his birthday of all days?"

"It's either now, Thanksgiving, or Christmas. Pick which one to ruin." He comes off condescending. And not like her, Gwen doesn't say anything in response.

*KNOCK. KNOCK. KNOCK.* Curtis jerks up. "I thought you said he was stopping by…"

"Maybe he already did," Gwen suggests, deliberately interrupting him. "I know you're anxious, but you need to relax the best you can."

"How?"

"Take deep breaths." It sounds like she's talking to Beatrice. The door opens, and his intestines cave in on themselves. Only a matter of time before he finds a random man at his celebratory gathering.

"*John!*" Mr. Murray, in the other room, sounds delighted. After audibly assessing his father, Curtis heads out to the living room expecting to give a reason as to why Isaac is here. But Isaac is gone. Then, a toilet flushes behind a closed door.

"How ya doing, ol' Curt?" Mr. Murray hops over Beatrice's toys to give his son a *macho* hug. And Curtis does the same by giving him a few pats on his back.

"I'm alright, dad." He replies with a sense of shame; that shame amplified when that bathroom door opens wide, and out comes papa bear. Literally and figuratively.

Mr. Murray tries to wrap his brain around Isaac's identity as he squints his eyes. He then walks over with hand held out. This gives Curt some hope, and even excitement, until his father goes, "You're John's dad, right?" Curtis' caved in intestines begin smoldering amidst the high-rising acid briskly filling up to his throat. A full-blown exorcism is about to go down with projectile blood, organs, and vomit spewing everywhere.

*'Just say you are. Read my fucking mind, Isaac. Please. Please. FUCKING PLEASE.'* His joints are shaking to the degree he's about ready to tumble over. He'd capsize, drowning in his own bodily fluids.

"No…" Isaac starts. "I'm Curtis' friend." *Dun-dun-DUUUN!* His father hears correctly, F-R-I-E-N-D, code for: *TROPICAL FRUIT.*

*'Come on dad,'* his thoughts ramble on, wanting to actually say these half-baked, nonsensical jokes to him. *'We'll get there fast and then we'll take it slow. That's where we wanna go. Way down in Kokomo.'* One of his father's favorites.

"What are you doing here, then?" To all intents and purposes, that doesn't sound as blunt and rude as the context may imply. Mr. Murray has a real question. A bastard of a question, but real. Still a bit backhanded, too, let's be honest.

"Um…" Even Isaac gets stumped. Maybe Beatrice can sense the tension for what it's worth because she's the only one to speak up among a crowd of corpses.

"Miiikkk." That's her way of saying, *she wants milk.*

Mr. Murray glances at her, and then around to Curtis. "You really wanna do this here?" He points his hand for a split second at Beatrice, who's mama is fixing her up a cold, white beverage. "With children at a fucking birthday party."

Curtis shifts his head away from anybody who is anybody. He goes down a mental list: *Isaac doesn't like me – CHECK. Gwen's frustrated I hijacked a family reunion with a pity party – CHECK. Dad hates that I've turned to the dark side, playing for one team versus the other. Shit, this is no different than being called a communist – CHECK. Beatrice is enraged with me that I kept her from getting MIIIKKK – CHECK.'*

After a hyperbolic stream of consciousness, Curtis heads for the door. "Okay." He doesn't care anymore, or at least doesn't want to.

Isaac rests his glasses on his shirt collar, eyes on full display; showing the perturbed reaction Curtis' quiet and abstruse meltdown caused. *"Curt!"* He calls, racing out the front door after him. But not before getting a few jabs in at Mr. Murray. "You really wanna do this here?" He parrots the man. "Dropping the F word with children at a birthday party? Get your own priorities straight before trying to convert ours. *Fuck you.*"

Curtis is storming outward into the dusking horizon, following the gravel road. Isaac darts after him, and does get a hold on the kid. "You're okay." He assures him, but Curtis' tears indicate otherwise.

*"FUCK EVERYTHING!"* He kicks deep into the gravel, stubbing his toe in the process. *"MOTHERFUCKER!"* He hops on one leg, unintentionally parodying someone who doesn't know how to operate a pogo stick. He almost dives face first into the embedded rocks, but Isaac catches him. "Let me go!" But the bear doesn't.

"You need to calm down." Isaac draws from experience. "You're giving him power."

"He's my fucking dad. What do you mean *power?*"

"Shh." When all else fails, he tries that. And some normalcy is re-established. Not all of it, but enough for the moment. They stand there being misted with an aura of serenity.

Isaac brings him up to his shoulders where Curtis grips the back of his shirt, and that feels like a blanket. He detects it at the same time Isaac's face and chest take on the texture of pillows. Curtis promptly wakes up in his own bed, gripping his blanket and face buried deep into his pillows. He sits up needing to wipe his night sweats.

He peeks at the clock through his finger gaps, and it reads _**2:33am**_.

# 14

Stu and Dirk are lurking about the town in Curtis' head, no one else occupying it at this particular time. They strike up decent conversation to keep them both distracted.

"You haven't felt hungry in the slightest?" Dirk asks.

"No. Not even thirsty." Stu adds. They're walking off into an open field of pasture where three horses are minding their own business. In the center of it all is a blue and white Chevy C10, the same model year as in Curtis' flashback; completely vacant.

"Where the hell are we?" Dirk looks up at the skyline and follows the haze wrapping the horizon, bothered.

"What do you remember last before he dropped you here?" Stu interrogates. "That's where I started experiencing disorientation."

"I was eating one of those shitty burgers," Dirk almost gags. "My vision formed wavy lines along the margins, and my stomach felt as if a million fire ants bit down all at once and dug into my intestines. The pain soon stopped, but I slid off and felt a splat. Then I was gone. I woke up here next."

"That's what I felt last!" Stu blares, as if having a eureka moment. "A splat."

"And?" Dirk pushes.

"And what?"

"What can you gather from that?" Dirk slides his fingers and palm along the Chevy, and soon grips the handle. "It's unlocked." He announces, opening the door.

"He must've drugged us with acid or some bullshit, and here we are." Stu answers Dirk's question, who had already jumped to his next line of thinking.

"I think we can use this to get back to town," Dirk strategizes. "He couldn't have driven us far."

While he searches for some keys lying about, Stu plants his elbows on the truck bed's rim. "What's your story?"

"*What?*" As if Dirk couldn't get more piqued.

"Why'd he choose you?"

"*Listen Stu!*" Dirk exposes the neck of the steering wheel where wires are interconnected. "We don't have much time before he returns. Instead of meandering around, help me get this vehicle started!" As cordial as he tries being, Dirk's outbursts are getting harder to maintain.

"*Ye-yes s-sir.*" A tiny case of intimidation causes Stu to fumble forward into the truck. "Sorry," he apologizes. "What do you want me to do?"

Before Dirk answers, a gargantuan swarm of clouds circulates in a descending motion in the pith of the town. An unruly strike of yellow lightning clashes against the dirt, sparking a curtailed dust bowl. Beyond the blowing filth is another human, just how Stu and Dirk arrived. He stands up as Stu reaches the halfway point to his aid.

When most of the dust settles, an older man with Isaac's weight proportions and body type limps toward Stu. He only has on three articles: a half-buttoned flannel showing his chest hairs, black socks going up his well-rounded calves, and regular white briefs. *"HELP! He's coming after me!"* He screams.

*"Who?! Is he younger?! Smaller?!"* Stu cries back.

The man has teardrops mixing in with the beads of his sweat. *"HELP ME!!"* He continually screams. He doesn't register a single word uttered from Stu's mouth. He instead grabs hold of him, accidently throttling him blue in a matter of seconds. Out of nowhere, the man is met with Dirk's fist knocking him to the ground. Stu recaptures his breath while Dirk helps the mildly conscious guy to his feet. Once back up, he's able to pace about calming himself down. Still, he can't stop his crying.

Both Stu and Dirk assess the bruises and bits of blood splatter covering parts of his person. "What's your name?" Dirk asks to use as a tactic, having the man focus on factoids rather than haywire emotions.

It takes him a minute, but he finally answers with, "Eddie."

From thin air materializes Curtis, marching toward all three like a flechette being shot out of a gun. He pulls a belt out of his own thigh, having yielded it from another part of his life. Actually, not just any belt; the leather belt his father had beaten him with all those years ago. The blood still fresh in dreamland.

Curtis is picking up more momentum with each step taken, on a clear trajectory toward Dirk. The constant stare of retribution never breaks from the kid, as he raises the belt declaring his dogma by the *LASH* it produces. His blood of many moons ago splashes amuck. *"You're gonna feel the strains you've put on me."* He hauntingly states, mimicking his father.

Dirk gets in a fighting stance. However, he can't get a good balance from the ungovernable trembling. This allows Curtis an even bigger advantage, like he needs it to begin with.

"*FUCK YOU, DAD!*" Curtis howls at Dirk, whose petrified reaction is donning on the physical features of Mr. Murray. Dirk's bone structure, body type, everything transforms into Curtis' father.

But Dirk still remains under the mask, even with his vocal cords having adjusted to Mr. Murray's voice. He pleads for his life. "*STOP!! PLEASE!!*" Curt rounds out a sickish grin, finally reaching catharsis from Dirk's begging and Curt's lashing.

*WHACK! WHACK! WHACK!* Curtis locks the other two in a powerful still of their bodies, allowing the maniacal psycho to repeatedly lash Dirk down to ripped tissue and dripping blood. Curtis then levitates with a self-inserting god complex visual. He uses his mind to mutilate the remains of Dirk's body, still sculpting his face to be that of Mr. Murray's. "You're gonna pay dad." Curtis callously speaks over the conscious, twitching man.

Recalling a vivid piece of his imagination, Curtis remembers the first encounter he ever had with Dirk. The floating god bobs his head, and suddenly, an invisible force with uncut fingernails scrapes Dirk's knuckles, and gouging the fat in between. The nails are pressed in so firmly that when Dirk struggles, as little energy as he has, they move in a jagged migration up to his joints where tendons start to tear. "*AAHH!!!*" Dirk squeals. Then, the nails stab into his jaw, and thus jerks of twisting and creasing transform taut skin into dangling veins.

For the finale, Curtis hooks something unseeable through that mighty thick rope of dripping nerves and flies Dirk to his level. There, he makes the bloodied man explode gushes of vital fluid out his ears. A force so graphic and cogent, a bombastic eruption leads to that of fissured bones, causing a sanguinary bidet to rupture from the chiseled shape of Dirk's mouth. His body plummets to the ground like an abused play doll.

Curtis turns his head with unbridled outrage, rainfall pouring down both cheeks, commanding Eddie's flannel to peel off. He then lacerates his underwear in two and slashes straight down the fabric of his socks. Eddie is left undisguised in all his unadorned flesh. However, a new disguise takes shape; a restructuring of his hazel-colored pupils into ocean blue. His head of hair recedes back into only a few tiny strings. The pillars of his cheek bones rotate mechanically like an automated massage chair.

His unclad body has waves moving up and down, generating animated vibrations, and this gives way to the dissolving of some of his weight to match distinct features. Eddie's disrobed being becomes Isaac's, externally that is. Isaac's costume is there to simulate his presence, for as much of a fallacy as it is. Eddie's heart is still the essence, still the spirit which inhabits this new mold. That's the one thing Curtis learns right there he can't replicate.

*"Why are you doing this?!"* Eddie speaks in Isaac's voice, bellowing a hybrid lament of grief and sorrow alongside his physical suffering. Curtis coordinates his fly down to the ground where feet stir up Dirk's blood soaking in the dirt. Passing dust causes the remaining three to violently cough against their hysteria.

Stu, who's yet to be released of his phantasmic chains, pulls on them with great force hoping to break loose. Curtis senses his desire for movement, and his antagonism building as if he's constructing an internal militancy. A precipitous lightning strike trickles down the blazing stars, tearing the skyline in two. This figure a hundred times more gargantuan rumbles through, making its formation known through its jagged heptagonal eyes peering through like a human over a colony of ants.

Curtis stares open mouthed, simply terrified and nothing less. Then, a tackle blindsides him. Two hands had gripped his torso from both ends, and threw him out into the open field. That huge splash of fear had forced him to renounce control over Stu, who can finally move about by his own volition. Curtis takes a quick glare at the nude man making sure he's still bounded at least, and he is.

He and Stu grapple one another with murder on the latter's mind. While Curtis is fighting with all his physical power, you can see he's striving to seize recontrol of the mental kind so physicality is only aesthetic.

The kid inevitably has to try a technique that seems erroneous, but the logic is there, or so he thinks. He recalls way back to when he and his sister would play the underwater game of holding one's own breath. Whoever could do it longer would win the game. *'Calm down,'* he told himself then and tells himself now. *'Let go.'* And so, he does. At first, Stu's joints are felt upon his face with the pressure weight of a ton. If it weren't for the next three seconds, Curtis wouldn't be alive half-a-minute longer.

Stu's motor begins to rust and glitch. He slows down to snail pace frames before becoming glued again to all his joints and muscles. "*STOOOPPPP……*" Stu's lips are the final muscles to stiffen, locked in a hold. His photo expression is evocative of a man who is about to meet a fate extremely violating.

Curtis uses his elbows to let his upper half rise, giving Stu a sweet and intimidating look rolled into one. "It's alright, Curt," the kid refers to himself in the third person, and that declaration not only transforming Stu's face into a Curtis clone, but ripping off all his clothes in one fell swoop. "Isaac's gonna love you." Curtis in a romantically evil gesture caresses the man's new face, and then looks to Eddie who'd been sat like a dog.

Stu's emotions are so uncomfortable, and his fears are so great, he's able to break a cry in Curtis' voice, *"GOD HELP ME!!!"* Immediately after, he's dragged along the dirt floor creating long imprinted slashes with his nails. *SPLAT!!!* Eddie and Stu have now become the drawing Curtis had been working on since that night at the bar. The kid can look at it, mesmerized in what he considers beautiful and exciting. Stu is oozing into Eddie, their bodies merging into one amorphous blob. And once that blob takes a lack of shape, their agonizing screams are muffled by the greasy fat smothering them both, who have now become one monstrous pile of jelly.

Steam begins to form and blood starts to percolate through all those layers of flesh, and this is symbiotic to Curtis' exhilarated fever as if this is the reason why the blob is seeping bodily fluids all of a sudden. And out of the blue, or red in this case, a great big splash of blood drowns him in momentary mania. *"AAAHHH!!!"* He kicks and screams, and then turns his head at the tear in the sky; that thing is gone.

A shape begins to outline itself directly in front of him, however; one of a humanoid template. Then another. Then another after that. Out of thin air, eight people manifest into being. Curtis rubs his eyelids raw, to the extremity of blood seeping behind optic apertures. He winces and blinks. These people have turned from glowing yellow lines to fleshly dressed ladies and gentlemen.

He blinks so much; he has a difficult time figuring if one of them is John. Curtis moves intermittently, walking sidestep to tripping on one ankle with the other. He loses total balance and goes fumbling on his back. The man in question steps forward, revealing that it is indeed John. "These people would like a word with you, Curtis." He states, having an unyielding and intimidating look.

A woman steps further out, taking the role of leader just by her gesture. She's cold and unflinching, calculating with her presentation. "We will be inaugurating your mind as the ninth territory," her and John move back to rejoin the collective. "Welcome to the Minds of Sensical Chaos."

<br>

END

GREYSON GIBSON'S
TELL,
CAN'T SHOW

Frederic and Isabelle gave birth to a baby boy. His name was Jackson. It was Thursday, April 5th, 2114 at 5:07pm when they had enough Exist Tokens to pay for a modified conscience. This conscience was an amalgamation of their thoughts, fears, dreams, and behaviors; each one costing 1,000 Exist Tokens. Frederic was at first leery at the idea of producing consciousness while Isabelle knew right at the start of their relationship all those years ago. She wanted an extension of them; a sort of prize to glorify their own matter, or lack thereof.

* * *

## MARCH 24TH, 2131

Frederic was in territory 9,743 of 30,000 when he began a dialogue with Bianca, who'd been approaching 134 years. It said so at the top of her charcoal-colored profile. In fact, all 521 conscious beings in that territory including Frederic had that same charcoal-colored profile. Actually, any being who existed in any territory had that profile look. All 23-million of them, and counting of course; as with the case of Jackson and others like him.

All there was to existence anymore were these 30,000 digital spaces called territories, with each one only able to house at most a thousand beings at a time. This was because each conscience took up twenty terabytes on average, and 24,000 terabytes were the limit per territory.

Before it became strictly sound, each conscience had eighty additional terabytes to them. Rendered physicality not only took up too much space, but would also buffer the realm entirely; all 30,000 territories. As a result, the governmental force at hand went strictly to sound. No more did conscious beings have outer shells. No more did they bear the costume of skin and bone. No more would they have to eat. No more would they have to sleep. No more would they have to thirst for water. No more would they have to breathe for life.

Beings could, of course, jump from one territory to another. In sooth, the governmental force highly encouraged it; so much so they implemented Exist Tokens. These were rewarded to a conscience who occupied a territory for at least twenty-four hours straight, and none of these territories could be that of the last five. These Exist Tokens were divvied out in amounts of fifty.

Frederic was away from his wife for some time. Both of them had gone off to different territories, hanging in each one for that twenty-four-hour window to claim those tokens. Frederic was approaching hour twenty-four with three minutes left to spare. He was almost ten for ten now, and would meet up with Isabelle in just a matter of minutes.

"Got any plans tomorrow?" Frederic asked Bianca, all other 519 muted and on temporary ignore.

"Existing." She answered, as plainly as anyone would in those days. Though her voice still sounded youthful and spry despite her age. That was due to a modification feature added in shortly after physical renders were done away with. Anyone could dictate the tone of their voice with these three categories: flow, inflection, and annunciation. However, at a price of 100 Exist Tokens per category.

Nonetheless, one could leave it on default when conscience was born, or created, as some preferred to put it. Default mode was just those three categories on an average growth development; meaning at three-years-old, they would sound like an average three-year-old. At four-years-old, they would sound like an average four-year-old. And so on. Frederic and Isabelle went with default mode for Jackson. Isabelle especially wanted to mimic the ancestral structure of human shells; how the vocal cords would organically mature way back in the 21$^{st}$ century and before.

"Well, same here." Frederic continued. He went on talking with Bianca, but it was more out of obligation than interest. It was a way to expedite time to make those three minutes flash by like three seconds.

"How's Jackson?" Bianca wondered.

"He's terrific," Frederic couldn't have sounded duller. "Going on seventeen years here pretty soon."

"My little Tiffany is just now approaching five years and…" Bianca was then interrupted by an impatient Frederic, who rose his volume over hers.

"I gotta get going, Bianca. Maybe I'll hear you around at some point." And just like that, those three minutes, which had sped up to three seconds, had gone just like that. And Frederic left.

Frederic and Isabelle soon met up in territory 1, the only territory which had unlimited storage. This was the government's space, where Exist Tokens could and would be spent.

"Did you get 'em already?" Isabelle asked Frederic.

"Give me a minute. Sometimes they buffer when you leave a territory too quick."

"You don't have to give me an attitude."

"Give me a break. Existing is hard work."

Frederic and Isabelle together accumulated 1,000 Exist Tokens. And with that they could spend 250 on each of them to lengthen their consciences; to extend the expiration date, which was superimposed on all 23-million charcoal-colored profiles. Underneath was a timer, counting down to the second.

You see, in those days, a being would need to spend tokens in order to extend their existence. Otherwise, once that timer hit zero, the governmental force permanently deleted that conscience like a finger snap. It was 250 tokens for thirty additional days of being.

"Where is Jackson, Fred?" Isabelle worriedly spoke. "He keeps missing these things. He always has his damn timer so low."

"I'll speak with him." Frederic simply put. This was so he could stop any onset of anxiety coming on for either of them.

However, Isabelle resumed, "It'll be your fault if he gets deleted from the realm. Why did you download your thoughts and fears into him, and I got stuck with giving him my dreams and behaviors?"

"Because," Frederic had a political answer to everything. "My dad downloaded his fears into me, and that's what shaped me to being self-reliant. Just couple that with my thought process and science will take care of the rest."

She, in a passive way, mumbled, "You speak so neutral."

In turn, he carried on with a more upbeat tune to his gab. "He got your dreams and behaviors."

"But fear controls all, Fred." She stated, with a provocative emphasis.

This caused Frederic to respond very bluntly. "What does he have to be scared of? We don't have illness anymore. No physical pain. Don't have to work. No possibility of unpredictable death. You only die if you choose to let the time run out."

Suddenly, another conscience joined the territory, Jackson. Both Frederic and Isabelle received a notification in their rectangular profile.

"Jackson's here," Frederic began. "See… you worry for nothing." Next, both he and her unignored and unmuted him.

And Jackson did the same, who then went on with, "Sorry I'm late. I was hanging out with Cynthia."

"Did you at least hang out in just one territory?" Isabelle was now in interrogation mode.

"*Yeeesss.*"

"Was it the full twenty-four?" Asked Frederic.

"No. I only did it for fifteen. I'll go back and complete it after this."

"*How many times must we tell you?!*" Yelled Isabelle. "It has to be a consistent twenty-four-hour stay. If you are to be trusted on your own, you need to take care of the most basic necessities."

"You never told me that!" Jackson went posthaste at them with a loud cry.

Frederic then chimed in strikingly nonchalant. "Yes, we have. Numerous times."

"Again, can you *not* be *trusted?!*" Isabelle irascibly continued.

"*Okay!* I'll stay in the damn thing for twenty-four straight. *Jeeesuuus!!*" Jackson went on mute afterward, ignoring any further comments made by either of his parents.

"Look at his timer, Fred! Look at his timer!" Isabelle pointed out. Frederic couldn't help but break a little of his calmness when he saw right there how long his son had.

## 02:19:34:23
**DAYS. HRS. MIN.  SEC.**

* * *

"We need to discuss something and make it very clear," Frederic came down on Jackson as soon as the two of them entered territory 21,228. "Your mother wants what's best for you, and so do I. We're trying to buy you a conscious sibling. But with us having to spend our tokens on your sorry ass, you're making it extremely difficult."

"I don't wanna start, dad," Jackson groused. "I've now heard this bullshit from you and mom."

"There must be something to it then. How 'bout you start earning some income yourself. It's not that hard to complete a twenty-four-hour window." Even though Frederic tried to squash any retort from his son then, speaking in an unpliable manner, Jackson became more averse to his father's demand.

However, Jackson did it not out of spite, but rather out of plea. "What's the point, dad? What is the *goddamn point?*"

It took a moment for Frederic to say anything. The silence he gave off sounded like he felt a cogent smite from his son. As if his custom reality had been shaken with a massive paradigm shift. Though the physical and visual sensations were not anymore, sound still carried emotional weight, and arguably more than ever.

"What's going on, Jack?" Frederic never called his son that unless he sensed an urgent feeling. Jackson at once remembered the first time his father addressed him this way. Jackson was seven-years-old. The year was 2121.

✳ ✳ ✳

## OCTOBER 3<sup>RD</sup>, 2121

Jackson's mother had been off chatting with her friends somewhere in a separate territory. He was just with his grandpa and father, who he called at the time Papa and Pops.

Papa had been reminiscing about the days long before these days we're discussing now. A damp fragility choked the tune of his voice when he'd spit out his nostalgic monologues.

"We'd go out with this blast, this gust of wind catapulting us across the house when we'd open a door or a window," Papa was romanticizing one evening. "The smell of barbecue brisket floated on up to the clouds where, in the skyline, this smoky fog was produced. The freezing temperatures made it all the worth when the arms of the flames would hug me in a comforting, radiating blaze."

Papa was the storyteller, and this retelling would be words Jackson never forgot; even down to the inflections Papa spoke with. It put Jackson in a hopeless state. It made him feel for the first time something was missing, and that something would never be reached again.

You could say Jackson was the ultimate prize; his mother thought so. Jackson was the trophy for those who fought prior. His existence was a glorification... memorabilia... a memento. He as his own figure wasn't real. His conscience was, after all, manufactured, handpicked, by the authorities around him. He was simply there to live out the legacy of his superiors. He was shiny though. But with that, the smallest marking of incorrect manner would drive his shiners to the brink of tyranny and madness.

Jackson wanted what his Papa had. What the man lived through echoed exploration, adventure, excitement. In the real world, not everything was settled like it would be later in this new digital realm.

Papa passed not too long after that, and this broke Jackson more so than it had broken Frederic. That last gasp of palpability soon vanished before Jackson really got the chance to hear the tales of real reality. *Trust me, I know that sounds redundant.*

"It was five years before they announced Project Existence," Papa started another one of his stories. "That would've been 2071. Shit… seems like ages ago now." Papa stopped for a split second regaining a concrete composure. But hell, those were *the days* of his life.

"Thompson and I at that time were together…" Papa looked at Frederic. "See, he was born in 2046, right? That would've made him just one year older than me."

"Yeah, dad." Responded Frederic.

"I miss that kid. He was my best friend," Papa lamented then. "Thompson was the one who encouraged me to join the digital realm. He had worked for the military, and was privy to inside scoop on this new invention. He ideally referred to it as eternal existence. We both were gonna join it. We both were gonna live this new world together. He got me in the prototype program, and he said he'd join not long after." Papa stopped again when this blubbering stutter of unbridled outrage erupted.

*"Why-wh-why did he-ee… have to get… get in th-th-that car wreck??!?"* Frederic would've if he could, put his hand on his father's shoulder, if he still had one.

"Where is the real world, Papa?" Jackson asked with laser focus engagement.

"It's gone, buddy," Papa put it simply. "Long gone. But… I can still feel. You may not, but I can. I can still feel that wind. I can still feel myself. And most importantly, I can still feel him. Feel Thompson. We truly were the last *real* generation."

"P… Po… Pops?" Jackson haltingly spoke. "Am… am I… *not real?*"

Frederic paused with somber qualms. Other times he would've scrutinized his father for degrading his boy so bluntly, but even he possessed a melancholic aura after Papa said what he said. This haunting truth permeated their charcoal-colored profiles.

Frederic, at some point, finally said something, but nothing necessarily reassuring. He referred to his boy as, "Jack. You are my Jack. You're real to me."

This yucky feeling infected Jackson's conscience then; the equivalent of a wet, frostbitten towel cloaking itself around Jackson's self-imagined flesh. And next, Jackson thought to himself he'd rather feel the pain of real flesh than just imagining it. Any sensation, good or bad, meant a lifetime's worth of actually existing.

Papa, with enough traumatic stimulation, began a novel-length speech. "The Government gave everyone until 2086, ten years' time, to transition into this new digital realm. Starting June of that year, they would be bombing the physical population. They justified it by saying it was economically, biologically, and chemically safer. That it was in the better interest of not only the country, but for the globe, to fully adopt and embrace this new world… *fucking liars.*"

"How long were you in the realm before you created dad's conscience?" Jackson kept on. He was imagining he had elbows, and that they were planted like stanchions to support his imaginary chin, which to him was positioned upright.

"Was it 2077?" Papa looked to Frederic once again, unsure.

"Yeah." Frederic concluded, and then he ended up wrapping that particular visit earlier than expected when he put his father on mute then. He could tell Jackson was spooked up and down and all around.

* * *

## NOVEMBER 8<sup>TH</sup>, 2123

It wouldn't be for another two years when a nine-year-old Jackson brought the subject of Papa up to his father. This conversation took place in territory 14,589 where this yucky feeling resurrected itself as soon as Jackson entered on through. After receiving the notification, Frederic muted any and all who weren't his son. This talk would be mounted as the catalyst for what was to transpire in the future.

"Pops, can I talk to you 'bout something personal?" Jackson began.

"Sure buddy. Whatever it is, you can go ahead." As much as Frederic embodied a stature of the all-encompassing reliable family dad, he would still be caught off guard with the vastly morbid topic Jackson was about to speak of.

"Why is Papa dead?"

"Jack. Why are you thinking that?"

"How come we get to live forever… and not Papa?"

Frederic had a slight pause before his next response. "Papa *chose* to not live forever."

Jackson, who was now lachrymose, gave a frantic cry. "*Why??!! Why would he choose to die?!*" Jackson tried to take a moment of silence, but his emotions were spiraling out of any sort of control. "*Was it something we did?!*"

"*No!!* Baby, I want you to get that out of your head. It is not anyone's fault. You hear me?"

"What does it mean to see a person? What did Papa mean by feeling someone? *Don't I feel??*"

"*Yes!! Yes!! You feel!!*" Frederic bellowed every word uttered. "You're just as real, just as loved, just as family like all the rest of us… like Papa was."

"D-d-did he not feel loved?"

"I don't know baby. I don't know. But whether he felt it or not, he was. He was loved. By you. By me. By mom. By a lot of people." Frederic mimicked that of a choking pause. "I think he just got tired."

"Are we gonna get tired?"

"We're gonna live forever. That's what this whole world is. A chance for us to grasp infinity." Frederic, with dreamlike theatrics, punctuated the end of his third sentence with spectacular hypnotism.

∗ ∗ ∗

## MARCH 24<sup>TH</sup>, 2131

Jackson's conscience remained elsewhere for a good chunk of elapsed time. He eventually did return to the present; where he and his dad were confronted with the burdensome veracity of Jackson, if it all was because of his own accord or by designed wiring. The amount spoken was just as much as what was left of the real world.

Until Frederic vehemently catechized his son with, "Jack. What is the matter?"

With ghoulish fixation, Jackson retorted, "Nothing. Nothing *is matter.* Not you. Not me. Not anything anymore." Jackson's voice was starting to give out. Maybe it was due to his quickly-spreading apathy. Maybe it was due to his slowly-disintegrating spirit. Whatever was the cause, it allowed for this impalpable parasite to eat the rest of his decayed conscience. It hurt him. It hurt him bad. And he wanted it to stop. Just stop.

"I don't *matter.*" Jackson tragically stated as he went up and down and all around. Up and down and all around. Up and down and all around. This vertigo-like mindset formed a flashing instability of all his memories; jumbled into one deformed, monstrous merge. And worst of all, he had nowhere to run from it. This is what he faced 24/7 as long as he was consciously aware.

The next thing Jackson said to his father would be the scariest utterance Frederic ever heard from his own son… because they both knew how sickly ill it meant.

Jackson's voice, now timid and froggy, played the tune of these dying words,

"*I'm tired too, dad.*"

www.ingramcontent.com/pod-product-compliance
Lightning Source LLC
Chambersburg PA
CBHW020611160726
47991CB00002BA/719